The · Newbery · Honor · Roll

SWIFT RIVERS

Cornelia Meigs

Walker and Company
New York

First published in the United States of America in 1932
by Little, Brown and Company.
This edition published by Walker Publishing Company, Inc., in 1994

Published simultaneously in Canada by Thomas Allen & Son,
Canada, Limited, Markham, Ontario

Library of Congress Cataloging-in-Publication Data
Meigs, Cornelia, 1884-1973.
Swift rivers / Cornelia Meigs.
p. cm.   —(The Newbery honor roll)
Summary: After being turned out by his mean-spirited uncle, Chris Dahlberg decides
to harvest some of the giant logs down the Mississippi River to market in St. Louis.
ISBN 0-8027-7419-9
[1. Logging—Fiction. 2. Frontier and pioneer life—Fiction. 3. Mississippi River—Fic-
tion.] I. Title. II. Series.
PZ7.M515Sw   1994
[Fic]—dc20   94-2339
CIP
AC

Printed in the United States of America

2 4 6 8 10 9 7 5 3

SWIFT RIVERS

Other Books in the Newbery Honor Roll Series

CONTENTS

SWIFT RIVERS

CHAPTER I

WHITE BIRCHES

It was the summer that Chris Dahlberg was seventeen that he mowed the high meadow alone for the first time. More than one of the men hired for the harvesting on the yellow slopes of his uncle's farm in the valley below had offered help; but he thanked them and shook his head with determination. He and Grandfather had cut the tall, wild hay of that meadow year after year, ever since Chris was a little boy trotting behind Grandfather's swinging scythe. Since, for some reason, Grandfather had not come down the valley this year to help with the harvesting, Chris was bound that no one else should wield a blade among the nodding grass, the sweet fern and the scattered flowers.

It seemed as though they always worked there on just the same sort of a late summer day, still and a little hot, beginning their labor just as the sun came up from behind the silent, forested hills to glitter on the feathery grass tops all delicately beaded with dew. Later, all the low ground would be flooded with sun-

3

light, the sky would be quivering blue, and the air would be so clear that Chris could see for miles past the woods which surrounded the hillside meadow. He could look down upon the floor of the valley, lined with long grain fields, and along the course of the meandering Goose Wing River to where the hills opened like a gate to some unknown world beyond. But he could never stop long to look about him, for he must keep up with Grandfather, working steadily with that long swing of his blade which ate through the tough stems like fire through stubble.

"Ease it down," Grandfather would say in his deep Swedish voice, as the grass rippled and dropped before his seemingly effortless stroke. He did not have to stop working as he talked, and so could tell Chris all about how that tumbled, disarranged place in the stone wall must have been made weeks ago by a bear, scrambling over clumsily to look for strawberries in the new grass. That dark speck which floated in the blue shimmer above the hilltops was an eagle. Then there would follow a story of the wary, wild creatures which hovered about farmsteads in Sweden, or of the bolder animals who used to dispute with man the possession of this newly settled region of the American North Country.

It was strange to be working there alone to-day,

4

White Birches

after Grandfather had always come so regularly on the first day of the harvest season. The dry hardness of Uncle Nels' voice seemed to take some of the sparkle out of the bright air of the summer morning, when he said to Chris, setting out up the hill with his scythe on his shoulder:

"Old Alexis Dahlberg finds himself getting stiff and feeble at last, I expect, and not able to lend us a hand with the work any more. Well, get forward, and take your gun with you. To bring back a few trusses of wild hay from that meadow which you and your grandfather call yours, that is nothing. But fetch us enough partridges for the harvesters' dinner and I will try to think that you are beginning to be of a little use on the place at last."

Chris had tramped off along the rough cart track which looped upward through the woods, his dark blue eyes on the grassy ruts before him, his blond head bent, and his whole tall figure seeming to be bowed by the burden of loneliness. Was Grandfather really going to leave him alone now, to do his work as best he could under the unloving eye of Uncle Nels Anderson? When he came in sight of the little meadow, however, that bit of open ground cut out of the close growing birch woods, he straightened suddenly and began to whistle. He leaned his gun against the wall, took

5

off his coat, whetted his scythe to a perfect edge, and began. One, two — he took the long strokes with the smooth rhythm of a dancer. He knew instantly how much he had increased in power since a year ago. He was almost equaling Grandfather's skill and, to his surprise, far exceeding Grandfather's strength.

It was well after midmorning, with a third of the field already cut, that he stopped to rest for the first time. Just as he lowered his scythe, there broke into his thoughts the sudden noise of crashing and trampling amongst the trees beyond the wall, the headlong galloping of some big animal. A deer — an elk even? No wild thing would ever make such tumult as that, unless it might be a moose, wounded and angry. But this was a horse, a slim, black creature, with an empty saddle and a broken bridle, which came dashing through the thickets to leap over the wall. Chris had never seen a horse jump before. The good cart horses of Uncle Nels' farm would have been as incapable of such a feat as of spreading wings for flight. That beautiful lifting of the head and knees together, that quick, agile bound, like a rabbit's, which carried the graceful animal over, where was there anything to be seen like it? The boy had seen deer leap like that, but deer were small and light compared with this glorious creature of grace and power!

White Birches

The horse stopped, wheeled, and stood for an instant knee-deep in the flowery grass. In that second a shot sounded from the wood, the sharp, thin crack of a rifle. Chris felt a strange, sudden jar which went tingling up his arm. The bullet had not hit him, but had glanced against the shaft of his scythe and knocked it from his hand.

With a snort of terror, the horse wheeled again and made for the lower stretch of the wall. Chris knew that to leap that barrier meant sure destruction; for just beyond it lay a long slope of rock, slippery with moss and ending in an abrupt drop many yards below. He was near enough, by being quick as light, to intercept the frantic creature, to catch at its black forelock and cling stubbornly in spite of rearing and kicking, of snorting nostrils and flying hoofs. Chris had stopped the big farm horses in just that way, but their heavy plunging was very different from the spirited struggle of this splendid thing.

The horse stood still at last, trembling, its dark coat shining with sweat.

"There, there," Chris passed a gentle hand along its wet, quivering neck. It was pain to him to see any animal suffer, even with fear. "But what is this?" he exclaimed in wonder, aloud, as though the horse could answer.

So close to the edge of the field had the struggle come, that, with the final plunge, a pair of saddle bags had been thrown over the beast's lowered head and had split against the wall. Curious objects came tumbling out of them, lumps of differently colored minerals; while there rolled almost to the boy's feet, two dark stones all shot through with shining yellow. They flashed in the sun as he picked them up. At the same instant there was again that thin, evil crack of a shot from the woods. A second bullet struck, with a vicious snick, against the wall just behind him. He dropped the stones into his pocket and, in one long stride, had reached his gun. He stood holding it poised ready to level at once, the moment a flash from the thickets showed him whither to aim.

He was aware, from the direction of the accurately placed bullets, that the shots had been more for the purpose of driving him away from the horse than from a real attempt upon his life. He was the more roused and indignant for that very reason.

"The horse might have been killed," he raged hotly. Slowly he moved out into the open, anxious to give some return, on his own part, as a warning to that skulker in the bushes.

He was scarcely prepared, however, to see some one appear, suddenly and boldly, in the gap of the wall

which did duty for a gate. The newcomer, bareheaded
in the sunshine, was evidently not far from the same
age as Chris Dahlberg, older, perhaps, by three or
four years. At sight of him, the black horse whinnied
and trotted across to drop its velvety nose and nuzzle
its master's breast. Without seeming to heed Chris
and his ready gun, the other bent down to smooth the
animal's black coat and to examine its straight, slim
legs. Chris, as he watched the youth's anxiety for the
safety of his horse, felt a sudden rush of knowledge
that here was no lurking adversary who would shoot
from hiding. He was across the meadow in an instant,
the gun in the crook of his arm.

"I think he isn't hurt," he began in somewhat awkward reassurance. "But he might have gone over the
wall, to break all his bones on the rocks below."

The owner of the horse straightened up to smile at
him gratefully, a quick flashing smile that was like a
glint of swift water in the sunshine. With his rumpled
dark hair and thin, clean-cut features he was unlike
any of the blond Swedish and German settlers of that
valley which held Chris Dahlberg's whole acquaintance. His clothes, a linen shirt and corded riding
breeches, were unbelievably worn and were repaired
here and there with buckskin patches, clumsily applied. And since this afternoon on the North Country

hillside was nearly a hundred years ago, his hair was cut a little longer than the manner of the present day, and always had the look of having just been pushed back from the boy's sunburned forehead by some recent and violent gesture. The two surveyed each other steadily as Chris let the stock of his gun slip to the ground. He spoke his bewilderment aloud, beginning in the middle:

"Then who was it who was shooting from the bushes?"

"Oh, did they have a shot at you, too?" The older boy held up his arm to show a long slit in his sleeve, evidently cut by a bullet. "I have been making a sort of exploring journey through these hills," he explained briefly, "and while I pitched my little noon camp down there nearer the river, some one must have spied Pharaoh here, and taken a fancy to him. Just as I went down to the stream for water, there was a shout from the thickets that stampeded the horse, and then a shot at me as I went after him."

"But we don't have thieves of that sort in Goose Wing Valley," Chris protested.

He had heard talk around the farmhouse table, of the law-breakers who drifted through thinly settled country, but who never had been heard of in this immediate neighborhood. This whole region was, some day, to be the State of Minnesota, but was now only a northerly corner of that vast tract, the Louisiana Purchase, bought just thirty years before by the bold wisdom of Thomas Jefferson. Even where settlement was older and closer than just here, there were no banks yet, or places for the safe keeping of valuables. Many a thrifty farmer's house might be worth robbing, or his choicest stock worth spiriting away. In this special neighborhood, however, there was not enough wealth to be very tempting to any of the hard ruffians known to be abroad in the more prosperous regions to the southward. Bears got the colts, sometimes, and wolves had been known to run down the young sheep; but of human robbery there had been no record. The Indians, the peaceable Chippewa, had moved away to dwell beyond the hills in better hunting grounds than these. They had always been friendly to the whites; so that never, through them, had there been serious threat against the farmers' meagre property.

"Hark," said the strange boy suddenly, lifting his head to listen.

The black horse was quieted now and had fallen to nipping the feathery grass tops standing so tall all about him. The air was very still as the two stood, straining their ears for any further sound. Far away in the wood came the small noise of a twig snapping, as though under a cautiously retreating foot. A moment of silence; then again there was a faint rustle and crackling of branches, farther away now, since apparently he who had coveted the beautiful, black Pharaoh had given up the hope of laying unlawful hands upon him. But who could it be, Chris kept wondering, since in all of his life in that small neighborhood he had never heard of a horse as being stolen. There must be more strangers than this one abroad in Goose Wing Valley that day.

The older boy dismissed the incident as though it had never been. "My name is Stuart Hale," he broke the silence suddenly, "and I was on my way to look for you, that is, if you are Chris Dahlberg. I had a message, and I was to find you here in the high meadow. That was where that splendid old man, in the cabin at the head of the valley, said you were to be to-day."

Chris Dahlberg's face lighted, as it always did at the mention of Grandfather. "Did he say why he did not come down to the harvesting? Was there anything wrong?"

"There was certainly nothing wrong," returned Stuart. "All he told me was that he had a fancy to see how you would mow the meadow alone this year. He said that when the harvest was all done and your Uncle Nels could spare you, then you were to come up the valley and the two of you would have a glorious three days together." He stood watching the glow of pleasure spread over the younger boy's face, and seemed to warm to it as he added, "I have been over your whole mountain range, looking for, I can hardly tell you what. But the best thing I found was old Alexis Dahlberg, in his house above the river with the great walnut tree before the door."

As though by common consent, the two walked together to the fringe of shade beside the wall and sat down upon the warm, rough stones. "I came down the road by the river," Stuart went on, "and asked the way to the high meadow of some men harvesting in a wheat field. The one who spoke to me gave me such scanty directions that I missed my way coming up the hill. We were hot and tired, Pharaoh and I, so I stopped to rest and water him, and that was how I came so near to losing him. I believe from what your grandfather said that it must have been your Uncle Nels Anderson who told me how to go."

Under his keen glance, Chris reddened. He could guess with just what surly unfriendliness Uncle Nels had turned away from the stranger who came seeking speech with no one better than his nephew, Christian

13

Swift Rivers

Dahlberg. "I have lived with Uncle Nels nearly all my life," he began to explain lamely. "There was a time of great sickness, when I was little, and it took my father and my mother both. Just before he died, my father arranged with my mother's brother — that was Uncle Nels — that he should care for me until I grew big and that I should work for him and help him until I was twenty-one. It is so, I am told, that things are often arranged, both in the old country and this. My father trusted him and Uncle Nels has kept his promise to give me a home. Grandfather lived here, too, for a while, but he and my uncle quarreled often and at last Grandfather went away to live on some forest land which belonged to him, at the head of the valley."

As the sun rode high above them to cross the line of noon, and as Pharaoh grazed comfortably in the shorter grass near the wall, Stuart, in his turn, gave a brief account of himself. He had grown very tired of hard study at Princeton, he told Chris, and had set out to try, "oh, a number of different things." He had tried a great variety, it truly seemed, for a person of a scant twenty years. His last venture had been a prospecting journey, looking for minerals amongst these northern hills.

"Oh," exclaimed Chris, suddenly remembering.

White Birches

"These fell out of your saddle bags." He drew out the two dark, yellow-speckled stones and held them out to their owner. "You found — that?" he questioned breathlessly. "You found gold?"

"I found fool gold."

Stuart took the stones and weighed their strange, flashing substance in his hand. "I was out for gold," he admitted, "gold or silver; I didn't have much interest in anything of less value. I may even have believed in the chance of diamonds and rubies when I set out, I knew so little about the whole matter. I stumbled on this and picked it up at the risk of my life, and I was wild when I found it, for I thought I had come on fabulous riches. But at last I collected my wits enough to test it, and found that it was worthless. The scientific fellows say it is iron pyrites, but the prospectors call it fool gold."

He was silent, turning over the lumps of dark mineral which glittered in the sun as though to deny his words.

"At least this proves that there is iron in these mountains," he went on, "but iron ore so far from a market is of no use to anybody. I think I have come to some vague idea that it is the forests which are to make the riches of this North Country. Some day the farmers will stop burning the big logs of oak and

15

birch and pine to get them out the way. Down on the larger rivers the logs are cut and floated to the saw-mills; yet no one in this new country seems to have thought that small streams in the spring flood will carry logs too. But I have no interest in chopping trees. Where would there be any excitement in that?"

He held out one of the yellow stones to Chris.

"Take it," he said. "They are worth this much, that we can each look at them and remember this morning in the high meadow." The glint of yellow gave a strange flicker as the dark substance passed from one boy's hand to another's. A smile that had the brightness of quicksilver went over Stuart's face as he added, "I don't see why you stay with your uncle, who is not kind to you, when you could live in happiness with that fine grandfather of yours up in the hills. Does no one ever see that he is growing very old? Or," he concluded impulsively, "why don't you leave everything, even your grandfather, and come adventuring with me?"

Chris had taken the stone and now gripped it in his brown hand until the knuckles were white. He sat in thought for a long minute and then shook his head. "I can't do it," he said. "Some day I will go to Grandfather, but not yet. And I can't go with you. The promise my father made must be kept."

White Birches

It was of no use to tell this new friend that there had been hard, struggling times in the Anderson household, when the burden of even one extra person had been great. Uncle Nels, with dogged honesty, had never sought to evade his share of the bargain, even though Chris believed so little that kindness and generosity had any part in it. Nels had no son of his own, his only child being Freda, two years younger than Chris and just beginning to grow tall. If the boy were ever to be of real use to his unwilling foster father, he was now coming into the years when it would be possible. Yet it seemed too much to try to speak of all this, so that all he could do was to repeat:

"It was a promise. I will keep the stone always, but I must stay here."

Stuart Hale threw back his head with that impatient motion of tossing the hair from his forehead. "Some day — " He checked himself abruptly, got up, and whistled to Pharaoh.

"But wait," cried Chris, feeling, with a strange inward pang, that he must find excuse for delaying this new acquaintance a little longer. "At least let me go back to the farm with you. Both you and the horse need rest before you start on the journey home."

"Home?" echoed Stuart, with a queer edge of bitterness in the voice which had been so gay. "There isn't such a thing as home in my kind of life. I got impatient with home; I thought I could come into this new country and win a fortune. But I haven't found it. Now I will be doing something else; there are a hundred interesting things still to try. But I won't be going home."

He swung himself into the saddle and was away down the trail. The sound of the hoof beats died away; the trampled grass began to rise upright; the sunny, softly humming quiet of the forest closed in about Chris as he stood in silent pondering. Finally he drew a long breath, took up his scythe again and moved to the place he had cut the last swath of grass. A clucking meadow lark ran out from almost between his feet; a striped chipmunk hurried back and forth carrying cherry stones into the wall; but he did not see them. The last surprising hour seemed to have left more behind it than just that strange nick in the handle of his scythe where the bullet had struck; for he worked on so wrapped in thought that he never lifted his eyes to look down to the valley, to the yellow fields and the silver glint of the river.

Only a portion of that reverie was concerned, now, with the question, why had Grandfather not come? It was only after many a fierce quarrel with Nels Anderson that old Alexis Dahlberg had gathered his meagre belongings and tramped away to the cottage at the top of the valley where the first white explorer in that region had set his dwelling. Grandfather had kept a watchful eye, even at that distance, upon his grandson's welfare, came to see him fairly often, and every year lent his tireless back and his long, swinging arms to help in the harvesting. Could it be now, as this passing stranger had observed so casually and as Uncle Nels had also hinted, that Alexis Dahlberg was truly growing old? As for the remainder of the boy's burden of thought, it was something which could not possibly have been put into words.

The sun was at the top of the mountains when Chris stopped his work at last. The silky grass lay in undulating rows; the stubble was sharp and stiff under foot. No person can labor for hours against the slight, obstinate, and infinitely multiplied resistance of growing things and not be very weary. But Chris Dahlberg had mowed the high meadow alone in the space of a single day, and he knew that things would never be quite the same with him again.

He was just taking up his gun to start homeward, when Nels Anderson came through the gap in the wall, Uncle Nels, tall and dark and in one of his black moods because the harvest below had not been so abundant as he expected. Across his shoulder Chris could look down the rough trail and could see, to his surprise, two distant figures ride out of the wood on one side of the way and disappear on the other. They were tiny in the distance; but even from so far away he knew that they were strangers, that even the horses upon which they were mounted, long-legged, rangy beasts, were no animals from that neighborhood. He was about to speak of them, but was interrupted by Uncle Nels' harsh criticism of his day's work.

"There is not so much here as should be," his uncle said, measuring with practised eye the little field dappled with piles of pale colored grass. "A better workman would have gone closer into the corners and got more."

"There are only blueberries and brambles in the corners," Chris returned. "Grandfather always said — "

"Give me no talk of that grandfather of yours," Nels Anderson burst out in fury. "Why has he not come to help us? I trust that he will be here tomorrow."

"I think that he will never pass your doors again," answered Chris with sudden understanding. "I believe he was only waiting until I was old enough to hold my own here, before he ceased coming forever. When the autumn work is done and you can spare me,

White Birches

I am going to him for three days. He has watched over me; it is time now that I should care for him." Without giving Nels Anderson time to reply, he shouldered his gun and scythe and walked away down the trail.

There was great commotion on the Anderson farm that night, for the best horse had disappeared, Brown Jenny, a good, conscientious creature with a little more speed than the other cart horses. Jan Peterson's gray gelding was missing also. It was alarmingly plain that thieves had at last penetrated the lonely Goose Wing Valley.

Probably the light-fingered gentry who had invaded that peaceful mountain country were not pleased with the quality of their spoils, for they did not return for more. The autumn passed with no further losses. Nels Anderson, who knew well how to keep people busy, seemed never to be at a loss to find tasks for his nephew. The boy rose earlier and earlier and toiled later and later, always hoping that he could clear the way to a day or two of freedom, so that he might journey up the valley to see his grandfather. No matter how much he accomplished, however, Uncle Nels' unsatisfied eye could always see something wanting and something still to be done. The autumn advanced toward winter, while Chris still worked without ceasing and totally without praise.

There was one morning when he arose from his bed in the loft and knew, from the harsh chill in the air, that the winter weather was not far away. He had made himself a promise that he would see Grandfather before the snows came. No matter what any one might say, now, he would set forth that morning, the moment the day broke.

As the whole household stood, in the gray light, about the great kitchen fireplace, he told his uncle abruptly of what he intended to do.

"The last of the wheat and corn have been got in long ago," he began steadily, "the wood is all cut for the winter, the cattle have been driven in and the hay and the straw are stacked. You cannot say that I am leaving you when you still have need of me. It is surely time that I knew something of how things are with my grandfather, and so I am going up the valley to-day."

Afterwards he tried to recall what Uncle Nels had said, but he never could recollect a word of it. He knew only that the harsh voice grew louder and louder, as the angry man's reproaches mounted to a very bellow of rage. It was on this especial day that he wanted Chris the most, it seemed; yet Chris stood to his ground and repeated sturdily that the really necessary work was done and that he had a right to go. Before this, he had often fallen into an agony of trembling before his uncle's rages, not from fear, but from disgust that a steady, sane person, who was kin to him, should turn suddenly into an unrecognizable, shouting madman.

But now he stood looking his uncle in the face quite unmoved by the turmoil of his wrath. He found himself thinking, all at once, that he had never noticed before how near he was to his uncle's height, even though Nels Anderson was spoken of as an unusually tall man. To his own astonishment, he discovered himself suddenly speaking aloud of these things. Since he had been to school and had learned English, he talked that language usually. But now he spoke in the Swedish into which Uncle Nels always fell when he was angry.

"You say that I am growing large enough to be of use to you; that means that I am coming to a man's size. Therefore I should and will have a man's place. It is not my plan to leave you after you have given me a home through all these years. My father and my grandfather and I, all three of us have said that I will not. But I will go and come to my grandfather's house as seems to me right, and I will listen no more to what you have to say against it. From now on there is to be justice for me, as well as for you. I am going to my grandfather because he needs me, and I will come back to you in three days."

He took down his sheepskin coat from its peg on the wall and let himself out into the early morning. The sun was not yet up; but there was a band of yellow light along the horizon above the dark hilltops. The farm laborers, going in and out of the bark-roofed sheds where the horses and cattle were stabled, looked curiously at Chris as he issued from the door with the blast of Uncle Nels' wrath pouring forth behind him.

With his hand upon the latch of the barnyard gate, he paused for a moment; for he heard light feet pattering behind him. It was Freda, his young cousin, Nels Anderson's only child, whose brown hands thrust a parcel under the crook of his arm while her voice said close to his ear:

"There are some warm mittens I have been knitting for your grandfather, which he should have before the winter. But Chris, however could you talk to my father so?"

She whispered low, as though, even here, her father's unreasoning fury would pursue her and find her out. But since Chris did not answer and only

24

smiled his thanks as he took the bundle under his arm, she dared to speak louder.

"He never lets any one talk thus to him, Chris. He will not forget such words. But even now, if you would come back and say that you did not mean it — "

"I did mean it," Chris returned. "It would not be true to say otherwise. Do you not know that it is right for me to go?"

As a little gust of wind blew across the farm court, her slim figure bent to it like the stem of a flower. She had neither her pretty mother's timid look, nor her father's expression of sullen ill-temper, but possessed, as Chris noted suddenly, a bright, firm beauty all of her own. She looked at him with direct, honest eyes.

"It is right for you to go," she declared, "and wrong of my father to keep you. But oh, Chris, take care!" She vanished within the gate as he strode out between the stone posts and came into the road.

So anxious was he to see Grandfather that he walked faster than was perhaps the part of wisdom. The whole journey was uphill, mounting slowly up the valley with the hills growing ever closer and the river nearer and more swift and narrow. He did not pause even to greet a friendly passer-by now and then, but just gave a hurried, "Good day, Jan Peter-

son," "Good morning, Marie Vicksell," as acquaintances went past. There was no dweller in the whole
of the valley whom he did not know.

It was toward the end of the afternoon that he delayed a few minutes at the house of good Eric Knudson and his wife Anna. Beyond here the road ended,
so that the way led merely by a trail up through the
woods to Grandfather's cabin. Anna was just setting a bowl of milk before the tired boy when her
husband said slowly, as he always spoke:

"It is well that you have come, Chris. I think
things are not so good with your grandfather as they
ought to be."

After that, Chris could sit on the bench by the fire
no more, but was up and starting for the door. Anna
made him carry the bread and cheese in his hand and
called out messages from the doorstep as he tramped
away into the dark. The wind was rising and seemed
to be looking for him as he mounted through the
wood. There was a wet, cold feeling in the air which
meant snow. He shouted at the top of his lungs as
he came up the final slope. Grandfather always heard
and came in haste to fling wide open the door of the
little cabin beneath the great walnut tree. Yes, he
could see the enormous trunk of the big walnut; he
could see the outline of the roof of the cottage; but

there was no light in the windows; no voice answered from inside. His legs were very weary, but he ran the last steep yards and flung open the door.

The bare room within was very shadowy, with only a glow on the hearth where the fire had burnt so low as to be scarcely alive. A figure moved in the big chair by the chimney and a voice cried out:

"Is it you, Chris? Then, quickly, take my gun down from the pegs. I saw a deer steal past the window, not a dozen minutes ago, and there is nothing in the larder fit for a hungry lad like you."

An hour later, Chris had a great fire blazing on the hearth, with a pair of savory venison steaks broiling before it. The poor, bare little cabin had turned into the cosiest and most comfortable of dwellings in the light of that warm fire. Or was it something else that cast such brightness everywhere, the glow on those two faces turned to each other in eager talk?

Alexis Dahlberg was smaller than his tall grandson, with eyes of a lighter and more dancing blue. He was telling, as the rarest of jokes, how his old enemy, rheumatism, had suddenly gripped his knees just as he was setting out to hunt two days before, and how he had crawled about the cabin, barely managing to attend to his simplest wants, and quite unable to reach the store of firewood in the shed.

"Eric Knudson would have seen, by and by, that there was no smoke going up beyond the hill, and would have come to help me in time," he declared cheerily. "But I might have had a cold night or two, before I was free of this demon which has taken me by the legs."

The snow began coming down in the night, while the wind roared above the roof. Little did those two mind it while they sat talking, long and late, as though there were no such thing as sleep or rest. Grandfather's lame knees improved somewhat in the grateful warmth, so that he could get up and move about the room a little to show that he was not quite helpless. It was at the end of an evening of that complete happiness which only comes to people who understand and love each other to the full measure of human possibility, that Chris gave voice to that same determination which he had declared to Uncle Nels. He had been stooping to mend the fire, but now straightened up to speak.

"I am going to take care of you after this, Grandfather. It is wrong that you should be here alone. Whatever comes, I am going to take care of you."

Old Alexis Dahlberg had struggled across the floor and stood now beside the window.

White Birches

"Perhaps you will have to care for me some day," he said, "but that day is not quite come yet. There is time to finish paying our debt to Nels Anderson first. Yes, we owe him a debt; he has done his part honestly, though not with any kindliness. This trouble of mine comes only once, or at most twice, in the winter. I shall do well enough from this time onward. And some day we shall be together, with never more any Uncle Nels to come between."

He was silent, peering out into the dark to watch the snow fly past the great, bare walnut tree. Then he spoke again, suddenly and sharply. "Chris," he questioned, wheeling about, "do you ever feel a wish to learn more than the little school at the crossroads taught you?"

In spite of his effort to keep an unmoved countenance, the boy's face flamed. He had gone to the small neighborhood school house and, further, had been taught in the evenings by a kindly schoolmaster who saw promise in him. Chris was not of just the same blood as the slower minded farmer folk of that region. That, perhaps, explained Uncle Nels' dislike of him. It also might account for his hunger for books and learning, a desire out of all proportion to the opportunities about him. He felt Grandfather's keen eyes reading him, and so tried to answer lightly.

They had been speaking of Stuart Hale, of his search for gold and his chance remarks that there might be wealth, but no adventure, in the project of cutting logs in the forest and floating them down the river to a market. It was to this drift of talk that Chris returned as he said easily:

"If we could turn these tree trunks, of which we have so many, into gold, then we would make this house stout and warm where you could live in comfort with everything you needed about you. And I would find some one to care for you for a little time, and I would go away into the world and learn the things that wise people know. And then I would come back to you."

He was putting a final log upon the fire, a big pine log which burst into a blaze almost the moment it touched the bright coals. As he watched the banner of flame streaming up the big chimney, he was aware that, within him, determination was burning with the same lusty fire. It was the unquenchable purpose to take care of Grandfather from that time forth, to make him safe — and happy, as he had not been through all these years that his grandson was growing to man's estate. He straightened up with the light of that purpose on his face, but before he could say a word, Alexis Dahlberg was speaking again.

"There is great work to do everywhere in the world, boy, and each of us must have our share in it. You must learn to do more than just to find food for yourself and me, and keep out the cold. Yet a little longer we must bend to the task of satisfying your Uncle Nels and then we shall see — we shall see."

The next day passed happily, but when the second morning broke, the skies continued to be leaden, with a fine, steady snow still falling. Old Alexis was now able to get about the cabin with a fair amount of ease, and, although scarcely any other man would have been willing to face the coming months of solitary living, he himself was quite confident that everything would go well. He was insistent that Chris must return to his uncle, for, he said:

"Nels Anderson needs you more than I."

The heaviness of heart with which they bade each other good-bye was covered by Grandfather's jokes and spicy comment and by his grandson's cheerful assurances that he would return before so very long.

"You see," he declared, "it was easy enough to come away, even against the wishes of Uncle Nels."

"You may be mistaken in thinking that," returned Alexis Dahlberg. "You have not yet seen how he will greet you when you return. Well, well, we must take men as we find them, Nels Anderson and his surly tempers amongst the rest."

Chris did not realize, until he set out, that a fierce wind was coming up, blowing sometimes behind him and sometimes flinging the sharp, fine snow directly in his face. The trail through the woods was somewhat sheltered; but the road, when he reached it, was heavy going, with the snow still too soft and light for snowshoes. He stopped for a moment at the house of Eric Knudson, to beg that he would see Grandfather often and would keep an eye upon his welfare until Chris could come again. Both Eric and Anna urged the boy not to try to continue his journey in the face of weather which was growing worse with every hour.

"I am determined you shall not go farther this day," Anna Knudson insisted and her husband, since Chris would not listen to the idea of staying, declared that he would hitch up the cart and drive him down the valley himself.

"In these drifts a man will make better progress than a horse," Chris told him with truth, "and I save three miles or more at the end of the journey by crossing the hill, through the birch woods and past the high meadow, instead of walking the road the whole of the way."

"But you will not get so far as the ridge path until nightfall," Anna objected. "Do you dare try to find that trail in the snow and the dark?"

"If we feared snow in this country, we would bide indoors half the year," Chris laughed at her fears. Anna was a young woman not long since come from Sweden, a simple, genuine soul who had kindness for every one. The boy set out, feeling strength and confidence for a journey of twice the length. Nothing could shake his determination to keep his agreement that he would return by the evening of the third day.

His cheerfulness began to droop, however, as he came, mile by mile, nearer to his uncle's farmstead. None the less he walked on steadily. The snow was falling less thickly; but the darkness was all about him as he reached the foot of the ridge path and stood hesitating. It was seven miles, around a spur of hill, to the Anderson farm, and but little more than three over the ridge. It was quite true that the path would not be altogether easy to find in the dusk.

"If I go over the hill, I may be in time to bed the cattle for the night," he reflected, and forthwith turned his steps up the slope and plunged into the deeper blackness of the forest trail.

The carpet of white made the dark less dense, but it served to hide the needed landmarks. It showed open ways, which the passing of a moose or an elk had broken through the brush, which looked like the proper trail, but which led nowhere. Twice Chris missed the path and was forced to go back. Before he had climbed half way to the top of the ridge, he found that he was hopelessly astray.

The straight, white birches which grew so thickly all across the hillside above the Anderson farm were quite absent here. Everywhere were twisted pines and poplar thickets through which he could scarcely make his way. He was beginning to be very weary; he felt his legs ache with climbing and, as he looked at the trees all circling, grim and silent about him, he seemed faintly dazed and not quite certain whether he were really going up or down. One thing he knew, that he must not sit down to rest; for the terrible lassitude of weariness and cold would keep him from ever getting up again. He struggled forward; perhaps he was even beginning to wander in a circle when something before him stopped him short. He had come upon the trace of fresh footprints in the snow.

White Birches

Since here were the marks of some one else alive in that empty waste, he followed them without further thought or question. The course of the way twisted and turned strangely; but all he could do was simply to keep on walking — to keep on walking. He was astonished, finally, to find himself brought up short, to stumble and strike his hands and knees against the rough stone of a bramble-grown wall. Beyond it there was a broad opening among the trees, a field — it was the high meadow!

As he clambered across the barrier and strove to step forward into the deeper drifts, there was a sudden noise of scuffling and scrambling over the corner of the wall. A dark form went headlong over it, carrying down some of the stones. He stooped down in the clearer light to examine the footprints more carefully. They were those of a bear, some tardy beast not yet holed up for the winter, seeking a last meal of dried and frozen fruit where it had fared so well during the warm, sunny months. Chris was on familiar ground now, for the rutted track down from the gate was plainly visible. He had no further wish to sit down to rest, but went striding quickly past the well-known curves of the sloping path.

It was deep night when he finally saw below him the steep roofs of the Anderson farm, where only a single faint light showed here and there through a loft window. The way was so familiar to his feet that he found himself coming easily through the untrodden snow to the great gate. He stopped in surprise, for it was closed, a thing of rare occurrence. Perhaps Uncle Nels was afraid that hungry wild beasts would be bold enough, in this untimely cold, to press up to the very sheepfold. Chris lifted his hand to the latch and stepped back in dumfounded astonishment. The gate, which, so long as he could remember, had stood open year in and year out, was not only closed but locked.

It was a great, heavy barrier of solid wood, built when there was still danger from Indians, set in the high wall between stone posts, and spiked at the top. To climb over it would be scarcely possible; all that he could do was to knock upon it again and again and to call at the top of his voice. He waited for long minutes; but there was no answer. One of the lights in the shed building nearest him went out.

Such weariness as he had never known came down upon him, the burden not only of a long day of hard travel, but of black and merciless despair. He was thinking dully that now, indeed, he must drop down and let the snow cover him, when a small voice spoke his name from inside.

"Chris, is it you?" The voice was Freda's.

"Yes, it is I indeed. What is the matter? Why does no one let me in?" he cried.

"Oh, Chris, my father said we were to bar the gate and no one was to answer when you called. But I could not bear to know you were knocking and waiting in the cold, I had to come down to tell you. My father says you are to go back to the mountains — that he is done with you here."

The boy stood for an instant utterly stupefied. He heard Freda fumbling with the bolt and finally saw the heavy gate open a tiny space.

"Slip inside," she whispered, "and we will hide you in the straw loft. You can be gone before my father finds you in the morning."

"No," he refused with sudden obstinacy, "if Nels Anderson has turned me off, then I will not come in."

"But, Chris, you are worn out and perishing with the cold!"

"It does not matter," he returned. In the depth of his exhaustion it seemed to him that it did not. "Go in again, Freda, before he finds you here."

A gust of cold wind blew open the wooden shutter of a near-by loft so that the light fell faintly down upon her, showing her against the snow. Sometimes Chris had seen partridges or swallows fluttering their wings so swiftly that the pinions became quite invisible and the slim outline of their bodies appeared in relief against the sky or the trees. Freda's erect slenderness always made him think of those hovering birds. The resemblance came to him dimly, even now, as he saw her stand in the opening, dark against the white. She spoke low, but every word came forth steadily.

"Sometimes my father decides things when he is angry and will not give them up, even when time has passed. He has barred you out and this is his house. But there is no one else here who wishes you aught but the best in the world. I beg you, Chris, to slip inside and stay until morning."

"No," he answered. His voice was as firm as hers, sharp and clear in the silence. He, and not she, reached up to catch the edge of the gate and swing it to. It seemed to take the last of his strength, however, for he stumbled as he turned to walk away through the snow.

CHAPTER II

FOREST TREASURE

Chris had no idea whither he was going as he trudged blindly away from the house where he had lived so long and where the door was now closed against him. Uncle Nels' gusts of passion were unaccountable; nor, when they hardened into cold decisions, did they often give way. Nels Anderson must have grudged, through all the years, even the food and shelter which he had given to a boy who was not his own son, with the result that a gnawing dislike had grown suddenly into consuming hatred. Nothing could have been more ill-judged than his furious decree that his house was to have no more to do with his sister's son. He had lost more than had Chris when the boy turned away from his closed gate; but of that neither of the two was in the least conscious. All that Chris knew was that he stood in the midst of a great waste of white and had neither strength to move forward nor knowledge of where he should go.

39

Swift Rivers

He had journeyed all day and had met scarcely one person traveling upon the drifted road. The storm had caught all the householders unawares, so that there was much to do in the matter of driving in cattle and banking the houses against the cold. It was scarcely to be believed, therefore, that, as he walked with uncertain footsteps away from the farmyard gate, he should hear a soft tinkling of bells and should see a horse and sledge looming large and unreal in the dark before him. He wondered dimly whether his exhausted legs would carry him to the side of the road, or whether the horse would blunder into him as he stood there wavering. Some one spoke, as the animal drew up with a sharp jingle and a man jumped down from the seat.

"Chris, are you safe?" cried Eric Knudson's anxious voice. "Wait a moment while I go up to the gate and open it so that we may pass in."

Chris muttered something whose substance he himself scarcely knew, but whose burden was an emphatic "No."

Eric Knudson, after a moment of dazed incomprehension, lifted the boy bodily upon the sledge and wrapped him in a bearskin robe. "Women are strange creatures," he mused aloud in wonder. "Here was Anna fuming and fretting that we let you risk crossing the ridge in the dark, until I had no peace. She finally made me get out the sledge and come to tell Nels Anderson that you were abroad on the hill, so that the household might look for you if you did not come home safely. Just to quiet her I came. And though you found the way, Anna must have been right, for there is certainly something amiss here."

Somehow, Chris, in a few words, managed to make him understand that Nels Anderson's house was the one place where they could not seek refuge. Without question Eric turned the horse about and set forth along the way he had come. "We will not try to get back to my own farm to-night. Anna will never look for that, but there are others will gladly take you in, wherever we may ask for shelter."

The horse went jingling along the track through the deep snow, which it had broken with such difficulty toward Nels Anderson's gate. Nearly an hour must have passed before Chris became numbly conscious that they had passed through a lane and had stopped before a door which now stood open to let out a flood of light and warmth, and of wondering, friendly voices. Just what account Eric Knudson gave them Chris never knew. The general acquaintance with Nels Anderson's sour temper and with his unyielding dislike for his nephew was probably explanation enough. Somebody was rubbing Chris, wrapping him in a thick wool blanket and burying him beneath an enormous featherbed, while a rough hand was lifting his head to pour a stinging hot drink down his throat. In spite of the confusion of talk and moving candles and grateful yellow firelight, he fell asleep almost immediately.

When he woke in the morning and sat up with a queer handicap of aching joints and stiff back, he could scarcely reason or guess just where he might be. But presently the worn, ruddy face of Peder Brask, the farmer who lived nearest to the Andersons, was bent over him, and he was greeted with a hearty good morning.

"So, you are beginning to be yourself again? Well, you must gather all your strength to meet the breakfast which my wife and the girls are making ready for you."

The boy felt uncomfortably and unreasonably sheepish under all this friendly care. Eric Knudson, so he was told, had set out two hours ago, so that Anna might be left alone no longer than was necessary. The bright sun was making cheerful yellow squares upon the floor, when Chris finally arose awkwardly. He peered out of the window, to see that the storm had passed completely by, and that the white·

hooded roofs of the barns and sheds were already beginning to drip along the eaves. Nobody asked him any questions, but every member of the household plied him with kind words and with evidences of friendly interest.

The good Brasks resolutely refused to allow him to set forth either that day or the next. "You should have minded Anna Knudson's warning," Peder declared firmly. "Now you must and shall mind ours."

Later in the day when Chris was standing once more by the window looking out at long blue shadows pointing up the road, the old farmer said gruffly, "I suppose you are going to your grandfather now?" and nodded approval as Chris said:

"Yes."

Within the boy's heart something seemed suddenly to leap into the vivid knowledge that he was free at last, free of that heavy promise which his father's necessity had laid upon him. Uncle Nels had never done him a better turn than when his unforgiving hand had locked the gate.

He was quite able, so he insisted, to set out on the third morning. Even with the snowshoes which Peder Brask had insisted upon his taking, he made but slow progress up the drifted valley. He had time to look about him as he had scarcely done in the haste of his previous journeying. He could notice, now, how the thicket of poplars at the first turn, near the river, had grown thicker and denser since last season, how wide was the spread of the great pine at the corner of the Jorgenson farm, how the enormous old sycamore which had stood so long near the summit of the Peterson's hill had fallen at last and lay headlong down the slope with its crumpled branches just showing through the snow. Sycamores are not so long-lived as other trees, he reflected. This one could not be within years of being so old as the great walnut which stood so strong and erect before the door of Grandfather's cabin. His determined face broke into its first smile as his wandering thought touched upon that stately trunk and those spreading branches and upon the recollection of how Grandfather always spoke of it as his "little nut tree."

It was in almost the first year that the white explorers pressed into this wilderness that the little cabin was built and the walnut tree was planted. The very first man to cross the mountain ridge and look down upon the headwaters of the steeply flowing river had known that here was the perfect place for a dwelling. Two smaller streams, dropping down the mountain side from opposite directions, united to make the clear depths of that waterway which the

Forest Treasure

Chippewa Indians had named from its crooked reaches, Goose Wing River. The tributaries came together just below a bold precipice of clean, red rock from whose summit the whole course of the tumbling river and the wooded valley was visible. For longer years than any one could count, the trails of wild game and of hunting Indians had descended the mountain ridges along the course of those two small brooks, and had followed southward by the margin of the larger stream.

When the first explorers set forth from Canada, it was with that idea which no man of their century could quite put aside, that those great sheets of inland water, Lake Michigan and Lake Superior, marked the end of the American continent and that, not far away, lay the golden sands, the nodding palm trees, and all the riches of India. After years of search, they were obliged to admit that they were mistaken and went back to their own land with tales of a country full of snow, Indians and great wealth in furs.

One man of them all chose to remain, not a Frenchman, so tradition said, but a pioneer of English blood. He built himself the cabin on the brow of that commanding hill, close to the highway of travel of elk and moose and red-skinned hunters. He carved out a

little garden from the jealously crowding underbrush, and, in the loose, dark mould at the top of the
rocks, he buried the thick-hulled black nut which was
to sprout with the first spring and grow into the
tremendous walnut tree. Of his children there was not
much told save that it was one of his descendants who
married, in time, that young Alexis Dahlberg, whose
restless spirit had brought him to the new country.

Many of Chris Dahlberg's blood, therefore, had
lived in that cabin before the time when young Alexis
Dahlberg, who loved travel and roving and the life
of a sailor, had become old Alexis Dahlberg and had
come back in his later years to the still, green solitude.
Alexis Dahlberg, so people said, had been everywhere
and had stayed nowhere, and now dwelt on his hillside only because an accident on his last voyage had
left him unfit for further wandering. For a few years
he had made the attempt to live with Nels Anderson
and keep an eye upon his growing grandson, but as
any one might have guessed, he and Nels had not
"made it out" together, and Grandfather had finally
taken up his lonely abode in the woods at the head of
the valley.

The walnut tree was enormous now, with long,
clean branches, each one as great as some of the biggest trunks in the forest. When it was a little sapling,

that first rover had sung to his children a song learned at some distant English fireside:

"I had a little nut tree, and nothing it would bear
But a little silver nutmeg and a little golden pear.
The King of Spain's daughter, she came to visit me,
And all for the sake of my little nut tree."

When the fruits ripened year by year, globes of silvery green turning to gold and yellow brown, the children who played below its branches still sang the song that first bold pioneer had taught them. And old Alexis Dahlberg, with his faint, wrinkled smile, loved always to talk of it as his little nut tree.

The snow began to be firmer under foot as Chris advanced up the valley, so that he seemed finally to be making fairly rapid advance along the twisting road which followed the river. On either side, the fields lay buried deep under their smooth blanket of white. With what heavy labor each one of these sloping acres had been carved out of the forest, with what toil men had tilled and mowed them, so that the woods would not creep forward and take possession of them again! Grandfather had had his share in clearing those lands, although his work had been broken by his voyages upon the seas of all the world. Grandfather's was a soul always thirsting for adventure. It was strange with what courage and patience he faced the quiet and loneliness of the life he must lead now. With every step Chris felt himself developing and strengthening that purpose of making Alexis Dahlberg safe and happy for such years as remained to him.

The wide door of Kaspar Gottorp's blacksmith shop was open, as he passed, with the red glow of the fire showing from within. Kaspar called to him to come in and eat, for it was nearing noonday. Chris answered cheerily that he must travel further before he made his midday stop, thanked his good friend without pausing, and tramped on, his snowshoes making their steady, soft shuffling in the snow. He was reflecting whether he should pause at Jan Peterson's house, or try to continue even farther, when a sudden turn of the road brought him upon one who was traveling the Goose Wing Valley also that day, and who had decided, too, that it was time for the noontide rest.

This other had come down that same crooked road that Chris was ascending. Instead of turning into one or another of the farm lanes to knock at some hospitable door where he would certainly have found friendliness and welcome, he had chosen to stop by the wayside, make a little fire in the snow, brew a cup

of coffee and fry bacon out of the provisions from his
opened pack. The snowshoes which he had taken off
were stuck upright in the drift beside him. The man
looked up as the boy came close, made a sign of greeting and said briefly:

"So you are obliged to take the road, also, even
though the going is none too good. Sit down and eat;
there is plenty for two."

Chris had been supplied with food by the kindly
Brasks, so that he could open his own pack and add
bread and dried beans to the meal. They sat on their
heels in the snow, on opposite sides of the fire, eyeing
each other, in quick occasional glances, across the
fluttering, orange flames. The man was tall and big-
limbed, and dressed in just such rough woolen clothes
as every farmer or woodsman in that region would
wear. His fur cap was pulled well down about his
ears, but it showed enough of his face to reveal that
his skin was of cloudy copper, scarcely darker than
sunburn, while his features were unmistakably that
of a red man. He spoke with a trace of French in his
tone and words, and he moved with lithe ease and
silence, as an Indian would. His fire was the small,
intense blaze that an Indian always builds. His dress,
his manner of speech and his easy, friendly smile
made it clear that he was, in part at least, a white

man; while everything else from the cut of his high-cheeked face to his moccasined feet indicated with equal plainness that a portion of him was Chippewa Indian.

When they had finished eating, he took out a small, black pipe, stuffed it full and fell to smoking. He asked Chris a few questions, putting his queries with the confidence of one used to authority and having a right to expect direct answers. The boy answered, shyly at first, then eagerly. He told about Grandfather; although he slipped over that dark passage of his life which had to do with Uncle Nels. He spoke of his determination to take care of Grandfather now; and the other nodded. That was how it should be, he agreed, but how was it to be done?

In courteous return, the traveler gave some scant information of himself. He was Pierre Dumenille; he did not live in these regions, very far from it. He was a pilot, a raft pilot, on the big Mississippi, some hundred miles away. Several times he had journeyed back into the hills to "see the people of my mother", but he had never taken the way down through Goose Wing Valley before.

"When you have learned to handle a canoe in these rushing mountain streams, it is not so difficult to

manage larger craft in the greater rapids of the Big
River," he ended.

It was very clear now who were "the people of my
mother", the quick, brown Chippewa who dwelt in
the woods to the northward, where the white men
had not yet penetrated, the red men who had no use
for horses but did all their traveling in bark canoes
upon the myriad waterways of their lake and forest
country. Yet as Chris watched him, he seemed less
and less like an Indian. There was something smoul-
dering behind those dark eyes which looked so steadily across at Chris, some depth of feeling which a red
man would never show.

The boy, forgetting his shyness entirely now, put
a pressing question of his own. If Pierre Dumenille
knew something of rafting logs, could he say whether
there was anything practical in the plan of cutting
timber in these hills and floating it down to the Mississippi?

"Yes," the other answered quickly, lifting his eyes
to the dark crown of pines which ran along the snowy
ridges above them. "No one has ever tried it before,
but some things must always have a beginning. Already logs are beginning to be somewhat scarce on
the banks of the great streams. This Goose Wing

River must be large in flood when the spring comes. But it will need a bold spirit to carry the venture over the first hundred miles. Once you get to the Big River, where Shreve McCloud makes up his rafts to send to St. Louis, then," — he flashed a quick smile which was entirely French — "then it might be my turn to take your wares farther, to the market at St. Louis."

He got up, showing himself of such tremendous height that even tall Chris felt small beside him. With the ease of smooth strength he picked up his heavy pack and settled it in its place before he slipped into the thongs of his snowshoes.

"Good luck to you, if you set yourself to this brave undertaking," he said. "May such a journey have better success than mine has had."

That dark, troubled look which had been visible in his eyes suddenly clouded his whole countenance. Was it because he had liked the boy's honest, open face, or was it because the pain within him was so great that he must speak out, to a total stranger more easily than to a friend?

"I took my way into the hills, trusting to them to ease a great hurt," he said, with queer abruptness. "I hoped to forget that I had quarreled with my dearest friend. But I did not leave that memory behind me."

Forest Treasure

He walked away without another word. Chris stood watching until a turn of the road hid him from view with nothing left but the long-stemmed ovals of his snowshoe prints in the soft white. The boy turned about and took his own way upward, his mind humming and buzzing with a cloud of new thoughts. Logs — the Mississippi — St. Louis! One glorious plan after another went sweeping through his mind. He and Grandfather would cut timber on these hillsides which were actually, in part, Chris Dahlberg's own; Chris would take them downstream with the rushing spring waters; he would come to that vast, faintly imagined river, the tremendous Mississippi. Its broad highway rolled past farms and towns and finally came to that city where all things were, even schools and learning. If he should journey afar on that great smooth road, what might he not find at the end of the way? Grandfather had fared on even farther voyages. Grandfather's blood and that of a hundred older Vikings ran hot in Chris Dahlberg's veins that morning.

He went gaily and lightly up the wooded trail on the last rise of the way. At the head of the slope he saw a figure moving against the trees, Alexis Dahlberg come out to meet his grandson. He had evidently heard from Eric Knudson of the affair of Nels Anderson, for his first words were, "So, that little matter is ended at last, and new things are beginning? What days we shall have — what days we shall have together now!"

Before the fire that night they talked a little of Stuart Hale and of what he had said concerning the wealth in this North Country. Chris told also of his meeting with the French-Indian, Pierre Dumenille, and his opinion in the same matter. Yet the boy said very little of his definite hope to embark on such a venture. He must have time to think it over, within his own mind. The snow had come before its time and presently melted away in the soft, hazy warmth of interrupted autumn. On the plea that he must get in meat for their winter supply, Chris set forth, a few days later, on a long hunting expedition back into the untouched forest of the hills and valleys north of them. He said nothing, even yet, to Grandfather, of how his real object was to examine the trees.

He marched and camped for a day and a half, in soft, Indian summer weather. As he journeyed, he met one or two friendly Chippewa, hunting deer and elk, and from them he learned more of the woods than he could ever have discovered alone. They, also, had need of timber, straight, slim trunks for lodge poles, wood for canoes, bows and lances. They could tell him of individual monarchs of the forest seeming to be as old as time itself, which quick Indian eyes and unfailing Indian memories had marked as the hunters went through the woods.

"We do not like them too thick," they observed, since primitive tools made cutting the greater trunks a difficult undertaking. In the mixture of signs and sparse words by which they could talk to white men, they told him something of that adventurer, Stuart Hale, who had been over much this same ground "two moons ago."

Stuart had come upon one Chippewa village, Chris was told, where all the people had sickened with a strange fever, so that the men could not hunt or the women tend them or care for the wailing children. The masterful white youth had forced the sick and protesting warriors to rise from their beds and move the camp to a high, windy ridge where clean water poured past them from a mountain top. The village would long remember the miracle of recovery which followed his efforts, nor would its men soon forget the scornful reproofs which, even with his scant knowledge of their tongue, he heaped upon them for setting their encampment in a wet, unwholesome swamp. In another Chippewa settlement, however, he had fallen into a fearful quarrel with a young chief who had thought him too arrogant and had vowed to have his life. Some of the older men, who had taken a liking to the white lad, forced the unwilling Stuart into a canoe and carried him bodily down the river. They smuggled Pharaoh after him under cover of the night and bade the boy take care that he never came into that neighborhood again. Chris listened, feeling friendship warm and strong within him, as he heard these tales of a strange young wanderer who had slipped in and out of his life so quickly.

He had gathered sufficient knowledge of the forest country, he decided finally, and set his face homeward on the third day. Eric Knudson was to stay with his grandfather for a portion of the time, but by now would have gone back to his own house. The boy at last made a halt for food and a brief rest on a rocky hillside, just where the woodland stopped abruptly and where the land beyond fell away in a barren stony slope. He was gathering wood for his fire, when a curious stone caught his eye, close beside the rotted branch which he had stooped to pick up. He moved from shadow into sunshine to examine the thing more closely as it lay in his hand, and felt a strange, tingling thrill run through him as he saw that it was shot through with brilliant yellow.

He looked diligently all about his feet, caught another tawny gleam and then dropped on his hands and knees to search frantically amongst the dry sticks and the drifted leaves. He found one more glittering pebble lying at the very edge of the stony waste, and without hesitation jumped up and ran forth upon the barren slope to search in blind and frenzied excitement for further treasure. It was gold, it must be gold! He resolutely refused to think it could be anything else. He had discovered what others had scoured the hills to seek, but had failed to find.

There was a strange rattling all about him, growing to a roar. The whole hillside was a slope of loose shale almost as unstable as quicksand. The stones slipped away beneath his feet as he fell and slid headlong; a great mass of loose rock sliding with him in a fierce clatter and a choking cloud of dust. He snatched for support in every direction, but plunged downward faster and faster, sprawling and helpless. He could not tell how far he might have fallen, when he brought up against some solid obstacle, with a thump that took his breath away.

When the dust had settled about him and the whirling stars had disappeared from before his eyes, he sat up very cautiously and looked about. The great sliding mass which he had brought down with him had split upon a solid outcropping of firm, red rock. Just below, but well outside of his reach, he could see a whole drift of the same glittering stones which had tempted him into such unexpected peril. He hung over the edge of his perch of safety and studied them long and carefully. They lay there flashing and winking in the sunlight. They shone with that strange, romantic magic which surrounds even the very dream of gold lying free to be gathered by men's hands.

He could not possibly reach the prize without trusting himself once more upon an even steeper and more insecure slope than that down which he had fallen. Many yards below, the steep incline dropped to a perpendicular fall, so that to step on that frail footing seemed to promise almost certain death. But the hard brightness of the shining yellow stones seemed to promise also the trail to certain riches. He never knew how long he hung there, weighing decision in the balance. Such a confusion of jostling thoughts went through his mind, prosperity, comfort and security for Grandfather, Nels Anderson's sour dismay and regret over breaking with some one who had reached out his hand to glorious wealth! Yet on the other hand there was Grandfather waiting in the cabin alone, an old man grown perilously dependent upon the presence of a younger and stronger comrade. What would be Alexis Dahlberg's delight on

Forest Treasure

seeing Chris come home with his hands full of the proof of sudden riches? Yet what would be his plight if his grandson never came back at all? And then for the very first time there returned to his excited mind the recollection of Stuart Hale's words as he had shown him, amongst his samples of iron and copper, the darkly shining stones.

"Fool gold!"

At this time, gold had not yet been found in California, the loose treasure which was washed out of river beds, news of which set the world on fire with excitement. But men were even then looking, as they had looked ever since the first voyagers stepped upon American shores, for gold which was to be had for the picking up, riches without effort. Chris reached deep into his pocket and pulled out that first stone which his wandering friend had given him. Yes, it was like the one he had just found. Yet in his first fever of discovery he had forgotten the very existence of Stuart Hale. What was there about gold which made a mere flash of yellow set a man quite out of his wits? Chris had forgotten everything, even his grandfather and the great, new venture, all for that sudden wink of brightness amongst the leaves. He had heard of one or two old prospectors who had gone, seeking, into these very hills and who had never

come back. Had they laid their bones at the foot of
that steep abyss into which he himself had almost
fallen? Had not Stuart Hale said something of risk-
ing his life for the possession of his own sample of
yellow mineral? He must have gathered it at this
very place.

Very carefully Chris studied the slope above him,
making out a small foothold here and there, a twisted
bush rooted in the stone, or a small outcropping of the
same rock upon which he stood. He turned about
cautiously and prepared to attempt the climb up-
wards.

It was a hideous journey as he crawled face downward in a long, crooked slant across the expanse of
the hillside. Once and then again he slid a few yards
in a breath-taking rush of clatter and dust; but,
spread prone as he was, he did not slip far and was
again able to make painful headway upward. It
seemed that he had been struggling for hours before
he finally reached the edge of the waste, laid hold of
a poplar sapling and stood once more with firm
ground beneath his feet. He could scarcely believe
that the sun had passed only an hour's space beyond
the high tide of noon, so long and perilous had
seemed the time which he had spent in that difficult
passage. His knees were trembling a little as he set

to the task of building his fire and frying his bacon.

As he traveled back toward the cabin on the hill, his mind was more absorbed than ever in the new plan of cutting logs, since now he knew what a wealth of timber grew all about them. Although he had talked vaguely to Grandfather about the great project, he had still said nothing very definite as to his steadily growing plans. He felt sure, as he reflected upon the matter, marching steadily the while through the silent forest, that he must come to the subject carefully, since any one so old as Alexis Dahlberg could not be plunged hurriedly into the idea of so great an undertaking. Chris might have to coax and persuade a little; but he was sure, in the end, that Grandfather would approve.

The boy was somewhat puzzled, as he came hurrying homeward up the last slope, to hear the sound of an axe ringing and echoing among the trees. Had Grandfather found need to cut firewood so soon? Chris burst impatiently into the clearing which surrounded the cabin and then stood still in bewildered astonishment.

Grandfather, stripped to his homespun shirt, was standing at the brow of the hill above the stream, swinging an axe with the same easy rhythm with which he could also wield a scythe. The sound of the regular blows seemed to come back from every direction, as the noise of woodchopping does reverberate in dense forest land. Every tree stem seemed to send back its small portion of the echoed sound, as though in powerless protest against the sharp onslaught of the axe. It could not, surely it could not be, that the rain of blows was falling on the trunk of the great walnut at the brow of the hill! Upon Chris Dahlberg's desperate exclamation, Grandfather turned about. He wiped his forehead, hot from effort even in the cold, as he spoke.

"I have thought much of that plan which sprang up in both of our minds that evening we talked of the restless lad who wandered this way looking for gold, and of what he said, so truly, about the value of logs. From what I have seen in my wanderings I am certain that there is more than one master builder of good vessels whose heart would warm at the sight of the walnut and oak, the birch and pine which clothe these hills of ours."

"But why — why begin with this?" Chris still could scarcely voice his wonder at what his grandfather was doing, and he added a further misgiving. "If we carry timber to market at all, it must go down the river bed. And is it not true that walnut logs are too heavy to float?"

Forest Treasure

"I have thought of that also," Grandfather returned. "In the older countries I have seen them float logs of hard wood by pinning them between trunks of something lighter. Two stout spruce stems on each side of these walnut logs will carry them easily. There might be a better way of getting them to market, but I do not know it." Alexis Dahlberg stepped back and looked up at the towering height of the big trunk.

"Trees grow old as men do," he declared slowly, "and this great fellow will become no greater. There is nothing before him now but, in a few years more, the beginning of decay. It is my belief, boy, that there are great things for you to come out of this forest, and that it is for a single good purpose that this giant has been growing so long. I may be wrong; but it is my wish to see, before I die, that golden fruit was really hanging upon these branches for you, and that your road to fortune sets out from the foot of the little nut tree."

Through the remaining hour of daylight they worked together, blow by blow, each swinging the axe in his turn, but were only half way through the great trunk by the time darkness fell. They talked by the fire that night and went over and over every aspect of their plan. Grandfather in his long wanderings had picked up much shrewd information and had seen, amid a multitude of other things, how the wise foresters in Europe cut timber from their woods without destroying them entirely.

"Eric Knudson will help us," Chris suggested; for it was plain that these two could not carry out so large an undertaking as the enterprise was growing to be. "Later he can bring his horse to drag the logs over the snow."

Grandfather went to bed that night earlier than was his usual custom and Chris followed him with great willingness. The boy had not counted on sleeping late, however, and sat up with a start to find the sun an hour high and Alexis Dahlberg no longer in the cabin. A strange cracking sound had wakened him, so unusual a noise that for a moment he could not identify it. It came again as he sat listening and was followed by a terrific, splintering crash. In spite of himself Chris covered his ears with his hands and sat motionless, refusing to let himself think of what had happened outside. Grandfather was right, even trees grow old and fall into dangerous decay. If the wood of the walnut tree were ever to be of use, it was wise to cut it now. But how he shrank from the thought of seeing that magnificent thing brought to the ground at last.

The door was flung open and Alexis Dahlberg

came striding in. Chris was used to thinking of him as an old man, with slightly shriveled skin, with a trifle of uncertainty in eyesight and walk. But for this moment he was once more young Alexis Dahlberg, hero of a thousand strange adventures on land and sea. There was a flash in his blue eyes, and a swing in his step which made Chris see him suddenly as he had been two score years ago, with all his strength leaping within him and with all the chances of a lifetime of adventuring still at his feet. He stood for an instant looking at the boy, and then all of a sudden seemed to droop and grow old again.

"Oh, Chris, have I done right?" he questioned almost pitifully.

"You have," Chris assured him with all the force of young and bold confidence. In his heart he knew that he would never have been courageous enough to cut the old walnut tree, but that it was the proper thing to do, none the less. The two ate their breakfast slowly and forbore to look out of the window. It was only when the last of the household tasks were finished that they went slowly together out of doors. It was then that Chris took command.

"Now it is down we must cut it into lengths," he declared. Cheerfulness came back with the music of the great, singing saw which they drew back and forth between them. They had launched their venture and henceforth they would not look back.

It was not until many days later that the great tree was finally reduced to a vast pile of logs with smooth, brown ends as beautifully patterned as a web of tapestry. The winter closed down with steady cold and with only intermittent bursts of tempestuous weather. It was astonishing how much persistent industry could accomplish, for the piles of logs grew and grew under the untiring efforts of the three axemen. Grandfather made up in almost uncanny skill what he lacked in strength; Chris had somewhat less than a man's full power; but he had gained ample knowledge of just how to make the most of what he had. And as for broad shouldered, broad faced Eric Knudson, he was an all-engulfing torrent of energy. Alexis Dahlberg used to say that the trees fell before his axe just as the tall wild hay would drop before the swing of a lesser man's scythe.

As the ground froze hard as granite, and as the heaps of logs grew great, the three began rolling them down the slope to the waterside. Those too far away for rolling were dragged by Knudson's horse to the edge of the stream.

"This year the cold works for us and not against us," Alexis Dahlberg declared with a chuckle, as though he enjoyed the idea of outwitting those forces of nature which, at certain times, had threatened to over-power him. Each timber had been marked at the small end with an iron stamp forged for them by Kaspar Gottorp. Grandfather had designed the shape of it, the rude outline of a spreading tree.

The weeks grew into months; the snow deepened and grew less; the twilights shortened and then grew longer. The turn of the year was past and the spring was coming.

It was a day in late March with the sun beginning to show promise of melting the snow and ice at last, that a most unfamiliar visitor presented himself at the door of the cabin. Chris, coming out with his axe on his shoulder, started back in astonishment on meeting none other than Uncle Nels upon the doorstone. The boy had grown hard and spare during the months of uninterrupted toil; but there was a clear light in his eyes and an ease and confidence in his bearing which had never been there during his years of un-loved dwelling in the house of Nels Anderson. The older man looked him over with a coldly measuring eye and came to the subject of his errand at once.

"We will have much work on the farm this season and I have not such good helpers as I should like. I will take you back, and say no more of how you angered me. I — I will even pay you wages now."

It was Chris Dahlberg's first impulse to throw back his head and laugh long and without restraint. Uncle Nels was offering as a favor to take him back into a slavery whose conclusion had been the beginning of real living for him! But life in the silence of the woods and with such a man as Alexis Dahlberg had increased his courtesy, so that he suppressed his laughter in time and replied seriously:

"I have come to understand that Grandfather must no longer live here alone. I am not to be hired, for I have other work to do."

Nels Anderson drew back from the door, as though his burst of anger needed extra space or it would strangle him.

"Other work! Yes," he sneered, "the work that can be done by a clumsy boy who was never worth the bread he ate, and an old man who has spent his years, just as a fool spends a handful of jingling pennies. I have heard of your fine schemes and how you are cutting trees on the hillsides a thousand miles from where they can be of any use. Your grandfather is always spinning his old man's tales of trolls and kobolds. He must have got you to believe that it is they who are going to carry your timber over the mountains for you."

Forest Treasure

Alexis Dahlberg had been sitting very quietly on the bench by the fire, listening alertly to the talk between Chris and his uncle, but taking no part in it, leaving the boy to come to his own conclusion. Now, however, he spoke up in a certain hard, clear voice with a touch of mockery in it, a tone which he used only when he spoke to just such people as Nels Anderson.

"So wise a man as you should know when words are being wasted, Nels. I bid you come in and partake of our hospitality and wish us well in our venture, for that would be more worth your while."

Nels shot the old man a coldly venomous look but said nothing in direct reply. He looked down the hill at the piles of logs laid all along the river bed waiting for the rising spring waters. He spoke slowly:

"If it is your plan to float that timber down the stream, remember, if you will, that I own land on both sides of the bank and past my place they shall not go."

"By what right do you say that?" cried Alexis Dahlberg, rising quickly and hobbling to the door, startled out of his appearance of calm. For answer Nels only laughed aloud as he turned about and walked down the hill.

Swift Rivers

All that evening the old man sat mournfully beside the fire shaking his head in misgiving over the threat of unexpected difficulty.

"Think no more of it, Grandfather," Chris urged finally. "The logs will not move for some weeks still, and when trouble arises with my uncle, we will find some way to meet it."

Grandfather brightened, though with evident effort, and at least said no more of his forebodings.

It was earlier in April than any one could have dared to hope, that the spring floods came at last. Chris could scarcely sleep for listening for the sound of running water, and could not believe his ears when, above the blowing of a warm spring wind, he finally heard the patter of melting snow dripping from roofs and branches. The ice, on which the greater part of the wood was piled, grew black and rotten. At the head of the ranks of neatly stacked timber was the pyramid of huge logs cut from the walnut tree, each one pinned by long wooden pegs between a pair of thick spruce trunks. There was some other walnut also, a certain proportion of spruce and a world of clean, sweet-smelling white pine, all waiting for the great moment when the water should touch the first heap.

Eric Knudson and Chris were to travel with the

Forest Treasure

logs, following them on their long journey down to the big Mississippi River where the rafts were made up and the timber started fairly on the highroad to waiting markets. The two were ready days beforehand, waiting impatiently to be gone. Anna Knudson had a young brother coming from the old country that spring. He and she and Grandfather were to live together on the Knudson farm. Since the journey might take a long time, Alexis Dahlberg had admitted reluctantly, at last, that he could not dwell alone.

It was on one of the evenings when they sat waiting and listening, that Grandfather spoke of Stuart Hale. "A strange fellow," he commented, looking reflectively into the fire. "He is the best possible company for a long, lonely evening, but he is a lad who, unless he changes his way of life, will never accomplish anything. A man may look for gold half his years, and fail to see other things which the world needs even more."

"Yet we owe it to him that we have thought of this plan," Chris returned.

"It would have been a plan of small value if left to him alone," Grandfather answered. His thoughts seemed to be wandering idly, for when he went on, it was to speak of an entirely different matter. "Once,

71

Swift Rivers

in my voyaging, I fell in with a man, a Mr. Barton Howland, a passenger with whom I used to have some talk in the warm evenings under the stars. He told me that he lived on the Mississippi, in a great house, I gathered, and with a host of serving men. He talked too of his beautiful wife. I am wondering whether the way you are going will lead past his door. I should like to believe that you will see him."

Chris replied somewhat absently; for his own mind was upon a single question, "How much longer will the winter hold?"

In spite of the excited watchfulness of all of them, it was Grandfather who first discovered that the chill waters of the stream had finally crept over the ice and reached up to embrace the pile of walnut logs. In wild haste Chris and Knudson made ready, gathering their tools, their bundles of provisions, and the little store of money which Grandfather had astonishingly produced from what Chris called his squirrel hole in the rafters of the cabin. It was Grandfather who, at the risk of an icy ducking, pushed the first log loose and watched it go whirling away in the tumbling current.

Chris, setting out after it along the rocky river bank, turned back for one last look at old Alexis Dahlberg. He seemed, as he had on the day that he cut the first tree, to have got back all his youth and strength and fire, as he stood there at the edge of the rushing water, watching with intent eyes while the huge walnut log turned slowly about in mid-stream and then slid steadily away upon its long journey toward the sea.

"Good-bye," the old man called in a voice as gay and young as was his face at that moment. It was not possible to tell whether the farewell was for his grandson or for his little nut tree.

CHAPTER III

GOLD IN THE ASHES

It would have been a matter of great surprise to Chris Dahlberg, chopping in lonely industry in the snowy woods, to hear that his venture was the subject of talk and wonder amongst his far-scattered valley neighbors. That community of settlers who had come from various northland countries, Sweden, Denmark, Norway, or Germany, had thought at home that the differences in their various blood was very great; but they found after they had crossed the sea that there was no great diversity after all. They became a friendly, united neighborhood, some of them bolder and more enterprising than the others, a few of them of less easy disposition. There were none who could equal the dour selfishness of Nels Anderson. They became Americans quickly; for they had much in common with the bold Anglo-Saxons who had been the first pioneers in the United States. They were seldom homesick; since this region of abundant lakes and swift flowing rivers, of white

74

birch and dark pine, was truly like home to them.

The long winters meant nothing to a race who had known snow and cold for three-fourths of the year since time immemorial. They had brought some of their smaller customs with them; the women still wore yellow kerchiefs over their heads and gaily embroidered aprons for festival occasions. They worked in the fields as whole-heartedly as the men; and the entire adventure of seeding and harvest was of vital interest to every member of every household. They missed some of their old country festivals, brightened by garlands and processions and dancing on the grass, for which the toiling frontier life offered little occasion.

A new venture by any member of the community was watched and commented upon with eager intensity. The experiment of cutting logs far away from a deep and navigable stream was a new and bold one whose outcome might be very doubtful. Yet each farmer along Goose Wing Valley had his own stretch of uncleared acres and was deeply concerned with the question of what Chris and Alexis Dahlberg would make out of this curious undertaking. Eric Knudson believed in it, or at least Anna did and Anna was the leading spirit on that small, struggling farmstead. Kaspar Gottorp, of the blacksmith's forge at the turn of the valley, had his doubts, but Peder Brask was sure that the two were doing well. Kaspar Gottorp was cannily glad to let the Dahlbergs have all the risk of the first venture; but he would be ready to put the axe to his own pine lands as soon as there was a hint that there was profit in the experiment. All too ready he would be, for Kaspar was of the sort who would cut his whole hillside bare with unforeseeing thoroughness. Nels Anderson, the largest landowner, the most prosperous and the most looked-up-to man in the community, was the only one who was completely against it.

"A child's folly, or an old man's, it does not matter much which it is," he told every one. "They are a pair who would be bound to find some way to ruin themselves. But at least they shall not ruin me, I am free of the responsibility of both of them."

Only a week before the water began to run free, Kaspar Gottorp came trudging up the hilly road to speak anxiously to Chris, cutting in the pine grove beyond Grandfather's cabin.

"I have no business to tell you," he said distressfully, crumpling his worn fur cap between nervous hands, "but that uncle of yours, Nels Anderson, is preparing to do you real damage. He has kept me working for many days on a great iron chain; and though he does not say what it is for, I can make a guess. It is his idea to swing it across the river so that your logs cannot pass by. If he should ever know that I had spoken of this, it would be the ruin of all business between him and me. He gives me more work than does any other in the Valley, for he has the biggest farms and keeps them up better than any other. But I had to tell you, Chris."

"He can't do it! He can't stop them!" cried the boy in hot defiance. But after Kaspar was gone, Chris Dahlberg's anger and resolution lost a little of their confidence. He had watched logs floating in a rapid current, and knew with what force they came plunging against any obstacle, to roll over it or through it. But Nels Anderson was a clever and determined man. It was strange with what heavy weight the thought of another man's enmity would hang upon brave hopes of success. Chris said nothing to Grandfather, but went about his work, wondering what should be done. The melting of the ice came suddenly. He had, as yet, seen no sign that Uncle Nels had dared to set any barrier in the way.

On the morning that the logs first began to run, the whole countryside turned out to watch them pass. When they caught against the banks or hung swaying on the rocky rapids, there was no lack of volunteers

to push them off. It was like some gay carnival, that
early progress of the long procession downstream.
There was laughter and shouting all along the upper
miles of the river, slipping and splashing as the untried helpers strove too zealously to assist the logs to
go onward, tumultuous cheering when a small jam
broke and let the dark, rolling trunks shoot downstream once more.

The biggest log of all and the one most reluctant
to travel in the shallow, swift waters was the first
section of the tremendous walnut tree. Through all
the long journey Chris was to find that great log the
center of most of the difficulty; on all the rapids it
was the one most prone to go aground; in the high
piled jams it was apt to be the foundation of the
trouble. But it was the one which set out first in slow,
stately progress down the clear run of the channel.
Some laughing girl from one of the farms had thrown
a garland of pine boughs and spring flowers to bring
good luck to the great enterprise. By chance the
wreath had caught upon the vast brown surface, and
clung there through all the first day of travel, spar-
kling with water drops, green and gay in the midst
of the hurrying tumult of black, jostling trunks and
white water.

The first day's run made no great progress; for

the river was not yet so high as it would be later. Then, with a sudden snap of biting cold, the winter shut down once more. The head of the trail of traveling logs had reached the pool below Kaspar Gottorp's place; but there the water skimmed over so suddenly with newly forming ice that progress was halted. The next day and the next were colder yet; the ice thickened inch by inch; and the whole journey came to a complete standstill.

Although Chris had waited the whole of the winter for the logs to begin to move, it seemed now that the delay of a single hour would destroy him. He walked some way down the river to look for open water and ended by sleeping in Peder Brask's loft. He got up in the night a dozen times, and stole out to observe the wind and the stars and the condition of the stubborn ice.

There was snow on the third night of waiting, snow which wrapped everything in the soft, wet mantle that late snow brings, instead of the hard, icy powder of the midwinter drifts. Chris, restlessly abroad at midnight, went to make the twentieth inspection of the hard surface of the river, and felt that he could not return to bed and sleep. For the first time he walked down the narrow path which skirted the bank and led to the farm of Uncle Nels. As he

came close to a turn in the stream at the edge of the
Anderson land, he heard subdued voices and a clinking of iron which, in spite of any effort for silence,
sounded clear in the stillness of the night. The boy
came softly through the snow, passed a growth of
willow, and stood still to watch what was going forward.

Lanterns were moving here and there; and not far
away one of them had been set down upon a rock to
light the work at the edge of the ice. Chris could make
out the burly form of Uncle Nels and could hear his
gruff voice giving orders. Two of the farm laborers
were bracing a deep-set post, and, on account of the
frozen ground and the impatience of their supervisor,
were making a nervous and clumsy task of it.

"Can't you make haste?" Chris heard Nels Anderson growl, shifting his feet in the wet snow. "The
chain is made fast on the other side of the stream,
and you should have got this end steady long ago.
Put those two big stones against the post; it will
have to stand plenty of strain." He shuffled restlessly
again, and burst out in desperate impatience. "Don't
you know that the logs might come down at almost
any time now?"

It was Chris Dahlberg's impulse to jump down the
bank, to strike amongst the three, to seize the big

sledge they were using and swing it furiously against the post until the chain was smashed free. But the weight of a great responsibility laid a steadying hand upon him. To do violence to Uncle Nels would not further his journey in any way; it might even put an end to it before it had well begun. He stood, raging and wondering what he should do, while below him the work was carried on with difficulty and hard words. At last one of the laborers straightened up with a grunt and said:

"There, sir, she's steady. I've done my best to do as you ordered. But I don't like it, Nels Anderson, we none of us like it."

What answer Nels growled was not audible, for he picked up the heavy mallet and struck it against the post. "It's firm enough," he said more clearly. "Now drive the last staple home." The clanging of hammer on iron echoed loud through the night.

When Nels Anderson was finally satisfied, he buttoned up his heavy coat and said gruffly, "Now you two are to bide here and keep watch. You can build a fire if you must; but mind it is a small one and under cover of the bank where no one will see. We have taken so much trouble, that we must make certain now that our work will stand safe."

He strode away along the bank, which was low,

just here, where an elbow of the stream skirted his most fertile meadow. The water ran close to a range of sheds where he stored hay and fed his sheep when the barns above had room for no more. Chris watched him disappear, but knew that the pair below could call him back, with all the other farm helpers, at the first hint of an alarm. He must wait, the boy decided, he must wait until next morning. The cold would surely hold through another day. In that time he would gather some of his friends and well-wishers, the younger men who had the most vivid interest in what he was trying to accomplish. They would come, a dozen strong, to the waterside; if they must use violence, then they must. Nels Anderson was not to stand in the way of what he and Grandfather had set out to do. He was sure some of the men of the Valley would help him, he was sure. So he told himself as he trudged back in the dark to Peder Brask's loft. He knew, in his heart, that Nels Anderson was a man of power in that small community. His belief that he could find men to stand against him was a cold, cheerless hope, very near to frozen despair. He crept into the hay of his bed and was so weary that, almost at once, he fell deeply asleep. The wind lifted and came booming up the valley from the south, but he did not hear it.

Gold in the Ashes

He was aroused, near morning, by noise below, by the sound of running feet, and the thump of a horse's hoofs as it was backed hastily from its stall. People were calling to one another in a confusion of alarm. The soft pat of the snowfall had given place to the drumming of steady rain. Chris plunged down the ladder to ask what was happening.

"Trouble down at Anderson's. A fellow came galloping along the road, raising a shout for help. Back, back, will you, Heisel. Step into the shafts like a good creature." Peder Brask bent to fasten straps and buckles in the lantern light.

Chris did not wait to help him, but ran, pulling on his coat as he went, down the willow-grown path by the river. The roar of angry waters which sounded in his ears began presently to give him some inkling of what Nels Anderson had brought to pass.

The ice, broken into great pieces by the warmth of the rain, had come drifting down from above upon the barrier, had caught on the chain and held, piling up in a great gorge and damming the stream. Water was spurting out on each side and flowing in shallow reaches all across the low meadow. Eric saw a little shed lift, lurch and go floating away, bobbing like a cork on the heaving waters. Nels Anderson's men were running back and forth, shouting confused directions and saving what they could. Chris could hear a big ram stamping and snorting in protest as he was hurried up the bank and the terrified bleating of a yearling sheep which had got separated from its fellows. As he stood still for a moment wondering where he would do best to lend a hand, he heard a voice call desperately, "Chris, Chris!"

It was Freda Anderson, dripping wet, her skirts snapping in the wind. She was standing on a great stone at the very brink of the river, with the water pouring over her feet. "Come quick to help my father," she shouted above the noise of the rain. "The others do not dare to come near."

He ran to her, splashing through the flood, and saw that the stopping of the stream had laid the river bed almost bare and that his Uncle Nels was down there among the rocks. He was striking at the wedged ice-cakes with a pick-axe, in a wild effort to make an opening for the water to come through. Chris jumped down beside him, took the heavy pick from his exhausted hands and swung it above his head for a smashing blow at the rotten ice. At that instant he heard Freda cry out again, "Look, look, the logs are coming."

The boy's mind seemed to move far more quickly than even his own conscious purpose could follow.

84

Gold in the Ashes

Without even looking up, he caught Nels Anderson under the arms and dragged him bodily to the bank and up its muddy slope. The water was swirling about their waists before they reached Freda's side. Chris had a quick vision of the great dark shapes of the logs, set free suddenly from the ice above, and riding down the flood in headlong phalanx. He heard a sharp report, half crack, half ring of metal. It was the chain, snapping like a thread under the onslaught, and whipping back to cut through the branches of a tree close overhead.

The ice loosened and crashed downward with a deafening roar; while more and more logs came rocketing over the crumbling barrier. The flood water about the feet of the three began to subside as the river poured back into its natural channel. Chris saw the big walnut log turn over and over at the crest of the gorge and then go shooting down into the deepening pool below. It was like some giant bellwether of a flock of sheep; where it could go, the others would surely follow. He turned down the river bank to set out in pursuit.

"Chris," Freda called, protesting, "you shall not go like this when you are half drowned. You must come to the house, to get warm and dry."

He glanced back at her from where he stood on

the bank below. Nels Anderson was staring at him dully as though still too stupefied to speak. Beyond, Chris could see the little shed which had been afloat, settling down crookedly upon a rock. Its sides cracked like those of a paper box, while the hay within came bursting out at all corners. He looked at the river and saw his logs moving steadily now, a well ordered army marching deliberately forward. He lifted his hand in good-bye to Freda and called through the sheets of rain which were blowing between them:

"Tell Eric Knudson to follow. I must go on."

Before he had advanced more than a few hundred feet farther, the veil of rain had hidden not only Freda and her father, but that hollow in the hills where lay the Anderson farm and the home he had known for all of his life.

Years afterward, Chris could have drawn an exact map of that twisting waterway with every pool where the logs tarried and lagged, every bar where they stuck fast, every rapid where they jammed and were forced onward, by sheer strength of will, in a furious avalanche of hurtling, black bodies. Sometimes he and Eric Knudson traveled together, sometimes many miles apart, one at the head, one at the tail of the long, floating army. At first Knudson paddled behind in the canoe which they had secured for the journey;

but there was a day when the light craft was caught between two shouldering white pine trunks and crushed like a robin's egg, depositing both travelers in the icy stream.

Later they used a dangerously large proportion of Grandfather's money to buy another boat, a stout wooden vessel, two or three times the length of the canoe, which the owner called a wanigan. In this they carried their scanty supplies and rowed after the trail of logs; or Knudson navigated alone while Chris tramped far ahead to keep abreast of the swimming leaders of his scattered company. Long after, he could close his eyes and see just how the treetops, swelling with spring buds, looked against the red of the morning sky, how the glittering frost lay upon fields of old stubble, how a silver bloom would show on the round, green hilltops when a shower of rain was coming. He was always wet, and nearly always hungry.

There was one day when he and Eric Knudson were delayed by a lashing storm of spring rain, when the wind was so high that the logs would only churn and plunge in the long pool of the river where there was not enough current to float them away. It seemed to Chris that he waited interminable ages, lying under the shelter of the upturned wanigan, overcome on his own part by an inward tempest of weariness and despair. Everything was against him, his own inexperience, time, the very elements themselves of wind and water, — how could he hope to fight them all? And when he came to the cities and the markets, what could a boy from the hills do against the greediness or enmity of the men with whom he must trade? But — there was Grandfather waiting at home, waiting, and believing in him. There was the desperate necessity of his finding success at the end of his quest, if he were to return in time to bring help and comfort to Grandfather's old age. He had to win; he would win. The rain and wind abated a little; it was time for him to go forward once more.

He and Knudson slept anywhere they could, mostly in the open, occasionally in farmhouses along the way, where some friendly woman would dry their clothes and feed them with her best. They had long since left behind them the familiar miles of the mountain valley. The river was widening, the farms were more frequent and stretched level on each side of the stream. It was surprising to Chris to meet strange faces, when all his life he had been accustomed to knowing everyone with whom he came in contact.

Sober-faced men gave him counsel concerning some perils, unknown to the friendly, honest community from which he had come. It seemed that pioneer life bred two sorts of men and only two, honest and dishonest. There were those who toiled early and late to win a living from the wilderness; there were those whose sole livelihood was found by preying upon the industrious and thrifty — desperadoes who could not soil their hands with real labor. In a region where a family's hoarded savings were kept in some secret place behind the chimney or under one of the stones of the hearth, it was no very unusual thing to hear of a stranger or two strangers as coming to ask for lodging for the night and leaving before the dawn with all that desperately won wealth in their pockets, and often with the blood of the whole household upon their hands. Chris remembered that nick in the handle of the scythe at home, and grew thoughtful as he trudged along the river bank.

He had progressed many miles ahead of Eric Knudson on a certain warm spring day. It had been very hot at noon time and he had lingered a little, as he stopped to eat the bread and cheese in his pocket, supplied to him at the last farmhouse. He hoped that Knudson would overtake him with the boat before nightfall, but feared that some logs going aground in a sandy bend had delayed his companion too long. When evening came, Chris broke off his journey, still hoping that Knudson would come into view, rowing down the river amongst the last of the flotilla. There was no farm within sight, only long woodland stretches of low ground with a crooked trail, grass-grown and sparsely traveled, struggling through the empty waste. A tumble-down log hut, which some wandering pioneer had set up hastily and then abandoned, lay half way between the trail and the water, with an almost obliterated path leading up to its door.

It was a forlorn place, with the stones of the chimney fallen in upon the dirt floor of the single room. But the heat of the day, and the rolling thunder heads, which had lifted above the horizon at sunset, gave promise of rain, so that even this dilapidated roof offered shelter not to be disdained.

Since the night air was chilly when the sun was gone, Chris, with some effort, kindled a little fire on the broken hearthstones. There was no glass in the small window, which afforded sufficient draft to carry away most of the smoke. Chris had eaten all the food which he had with him and must go supper-less to bed, so ordinary an event that he thought nothing of it. He was examining the dirty room, wondering which would be the best corner to select for a bed when he heard voices in the path. The flimsy door was thrust back as two men stooped their heads to step over the threshold. Chris turned about from the hearth to look at them and waited, a little uncomfortable under their intense stare. Since they said nothing he finally spoke:

"It's not much of a shelter; but it will keep off some of the rain. Will you come up to the fire?"

There seemed to him nothing very notable about his pair of travelers except for the fact that they stood looking at him so steadily and did not come forward to the warmth of the blaze. One was smaller than the other and neater in his dress. They were both travel worn and dusty, and both had the dark color of long-continued sunburn. The biggest one shifted his feet and stared silently at Chris, while the other spoke in a light, dry voice, rather different from anything the boy had ever heard before:

"We won't stop, I thank you, though you do seem to have found a snug little place for the night. We're looking for a fellow; we thought when we saw your light that he might have come in here. Have you met up with any one coming along this trail, youngish, a year or two older than you perhaps? He has black hair and a kind of a white face, about your height, talks sort of above himself, like he'd been to school somewheres?"

Chris had encountered no one in the last half day of his journey and told them so.

"He was to meet us here." The bigger, darker man spoke finally. "I don't know what's happened that he hasn't caught us up. But we'll find him."

They both turned about, but the first looked over his shoulder to speak to Chris again as they went out. "If you should come across him, tell him we're looking for him, and that we're sure to find him."

"Will you tell me his name, so that I can know whether I meet the right one?" Chris asked. "Or who shall I say were the men who were looking for him?"

"Oh, that doesn't signify," the other answered easily. "A white face, and black hair, he had, and when you meet him, he'll look pretty well beat out, because he's come far, and on foot. You can tell him we've gone ahead slowly, but we're still in the neighborhood. Buying cattle we are," he concluded in explanation, "and traveling through the country. We're sure to find him somewheres."

As they went out, Chris followed to the doorway and stood looking after them. Three horses were tethered to the bushes at some little distance. He watched them mount and ride away, leading the third horse which was laden with a packsaddle. And as he saw them moving off, he knew suddenly that he had caught sight of them before, had seen them, small and distant, crossing the wood trail which led down from the high meadow, the day he had met Stuart Hale, the day brown Jenny had disappeared. More than that, the pack horse lumbering behind them was brown Jenny herself. But it was scarcely the part of wisdom to go in pursuit!

They vanished down the shadowy path, where the woods on each side were settling down from the small, busy noises of the day to the softer rustling sounds of the night. Chris could hear their feet and their voices as they made their way back to the main trail; he could hear the creak of their saddles and the diminishing hoof beats as they rode away. The sound had scarcely come to an end when the door was thrown back once more and some one stumbled into the dark little room.

The fire, after its first blaze among the dry sticks, had dropped to coals so that the place was too dusky for the boy to see anything but the dark figure which came bursting in.

But when a voice cried out, "Chris, Chris Dahlberg, is it you? Can I stay here with you, can I go on with you?" he recognized it instantly. Although months had passed, he still had vivid recollection of that cheery stranger who had come up the hill to find

93

him the morning he mowed the high meadow. It was Stuart Hale.

The only act of hospitality which Chris could perform, by way of welcoming his friend to that forlorn hovel, was to blow up the fire and add fresh fuel. By its light he could see that Stuart was even as the men had said, white faced with hunger and weariness, and haggard with some strange anxiety. His clothes were dirty and ragged; one shoulder showed through a slit in his sleeve where, only but now, a branch had torn the rotten fabric and ploughed the sunburned skin. The older boy sat down and spread his hands eagerly to the bright blaze. For a long time he said nothing, either to explain his presence or to tell Chris how he had known that he would find him there.

But as the black dark finally fell, and the quivering voice of a little tree toad began to shrill in the peaceful quiet outside, Stuart Hale began at last to give halting account of what had happened.

"I have done so many things," he said, trying to speak casually. "Prospecting didn't seem to offer anything, so I have not gone any further with it. I tried this thing and the other; but I get tired of working steadily. And so I got rather down on my luck."

He had been ill and, in truth, nearly starved, so his

Gold in the Ashes

account continued, when he fell in with two men who befriended him. Henry Rhodes and Tom Loomis were the names they gave him and, so they said, they were traveling through the country "buying cattle." They lent him money and furnished him with food and were cordially pressing in their invitation that that he should travel with them. "As I didn't have anywhere particular to go, and as they picked up an extra horse about then, I was glad to ride along with them. I had sold Pharaoh; I got as low as parting with my last real friend."

Chris pressed no questions but waited quietly for the rest to come.

"I saw pretty soon that they weren't buying any cattle," Stuart went on, "but I think it was because I was stupid with being hungry and sick for so long, that I didn't understand for a while what they were. I've been a wanderer and I've liked adventures and I've fretted over plodding along at steady work, and I've seen all sorts of people. I ought to have known how those two were going about it to get their living, and why they wanted a third man to help them. By the second day, when my head cleared, I saw what they were about. They were talking together about a place up in the hills, and a man who was reported to have sold sheep for a good price and to be coming home by

95

a certain road on a certain day. But I hadn't got all my wits about me even then; for I was fool enough to stop still in the road and tell them what I thought and that I was going to leave them.

"The big one let drive at me with his pistol, but he is a clumsy marksman and the bullet only grazed the horse's neck. The beast plunged and reared, but I threw myself off him and got into the woods. Loomis held the hurt horse while Henry Rhodes came riding among the trees after me. But his beast stumbled on a root and came down, throwing Henry over his head. He got up and went limping and cursing back to the trail, while Loomis, that's the smaller one, sent a bullet after me. Mercifully it glanced on a tree. He isn't a man to miss usually. They stood there debating in the road, but the horse was bleeding and they didn't want to lose him, after they had been to the trouble of stealing him, so they gave up trying to follow. I went five miles or more through the woods and began to breathe easy, I thought they had given me up for good."

But when he sought shelter that night at a farmhouse, so Stuart's narrative went on, the two rode up an hour afterward and asked for lodging also. They gave no sign of having seen Stuart before, and sat with him at the supper table talking of the cattle they were going to buy. That night the three lay together in uneasy comradeship about the fire and rose up together in the morning, still with the bearing of strangers.

The talk at the supper table had all been of the experiment in log running, of which everyone up and down the river was now beginning to speak. The farmer tried to recall the name of the young man who was trying this new bold thing, Christian Dahlberg, wasn't it? Stuart jumped; had the fellow and his logs passed that way, he asked quickly. No, he was told, the news had run ahead, and the log drive was still a day's journey or more upstream. The two cattle buyers asked various questions concerning the enterprise until the farmer let fall the observation, "It's a brave thing for a young man without a penny to set out on such a journey." Chris and his logs held no interest for the strangers thereafter.

When the two men set out, Loomis managed to speak in an undertone to Stuart.

"We'll be in this neighborhood for some time. You will be coming with us after all." Then he mounted his horse and they rode away. While Stuart was hesitating over the question of whether he should hint to his host what manner of men he had been entertaining, the farmer himself opened the subject abruptly by telling the young man that he liked the quality of none of his visitors and that he had better be gone after the others.

"My wife saw there was something between you, the minute you looked at each other," he vowed. "I'm not one ever to turn an honest man away, but I don't like the looks of any of this business." And since Stuart had nothing with which to accuse his former comrades which could be proved, he could not do other than depart as the farmer bade him. His one thought thereafter was his desire to meet Chris. Although he could not say so even to himself, his despairing mind evidently clung to the idea of what refreshing good it would do him to see the clear, honest eyes and the frank, sunburned face of the boy he had met on the hill, the boy who would not leave the house where he was unhappy, because "it was a promise."

Chris himself had longed to see Stuart Hale again. He wanted to tell him how a word of his careless talk concerning the possibility of taking timber to market down the Goose Wing River had borne unexpected fruit. And also he wished to recount that adventure into which he had fallen in the pursuit of the fool gold. They sat talking by the fire, hungry and tired, but quite unconscious of everything save that each

Gold in the Ashes

had been lonely and had found a friend. Chris drew out the fragment of stone shot with yellow mineral to show Stuart that he still carried it.

Stuart pulled its fellow from his own pocket. "I keep it to remind myself that I almost lost my life trying to get something that was perfectly worthless," he said. He, too, had had a similar adventure on the same hill, which he fell to describing. The boys laid the two lumps of stone upon the hearth to compare them and to laugh at their glitter which was still so deceiving. Stuart was in the midst of his narrative, when Chris lifted his hand in a gesture of terrified warning and the other boy stopped dead in the middle of a word.

"They're coming back," Chris whispered below his breath and the two sat looking at each other in frozen silence.

Only ears used to the quiet of the forest and its soft background of faint rustlings could, perhaps, have caught the first murmur of distant voices. But presently the sounds became louder, a light, dry voice and a deeper one, as feet approached through the grass toward the door. The noise of talking was loud outside, and the thick boots trod heavily as they came near. The two boys looked at each other desperately in the uncertain light. The only window was beside the door and in full view of the oncoming men.

There was a split in the rickety chimney, letting in the light of the stars, and showing well above their heads. Chris motioned to it, for neither of the two dared to speak aloud. He stood up silently, braced one shoulder against the wall and signed to Stuart to mount upon his bent knee, from there to his other shoulder and so gain a foothold between the gaping stones. Once up, Stuart leaned over to help Chris up after him. The whole maneuver was completed in the space of a few seconds.

It was certainly not accomplished in silence, but when the stones slipped and let fall a scattering of mortar on the hearth below, the noise was drowned by the voices without, for those who were approaching seemed both to be in ugly tempers. A gust of soft wind ran through the wood and slammed the rickety door almost as the men pushed in. Under cover of that crash the boys jumped down and slipped away toward the river. They looked back apprehensively for signs of pursuit, but no one came.

The breeze bore the noise of disputing voices loudly upraised, but not the rustle of following footsteps. Yet the two half walked, half ran, for a whole mile along the river bank before they stopped to draw breath. It was not the fact that the men behind them were armed and menacing which lent such speed and distance to their flight. It was the very foulness of their presence which made the two boys feel that a mile of clean, flowing river could scarcely make them seem sufficiently far away.

In Chris Dahlberg's ears there still seemed to sound that thin, hard voice: "Tell him we will be sure to find him." They did not look like desperadoes; they looked cheap and commonplace, as dishonest men so often do. But how good it was to be quit of them and of the sinister thought of their very being!

The boys must have tramped five miles through the dark before they finally paused for real rest. The flurry of rain had passed, leaving wet leaves to drip softly upon them as they brushed by. The dull sheen of the river guided them as they followed its windings, led by its hushed voice when some detour through the underbrush carried them out of sight of it. Now the stars were rippling on its surface and the utter hush of the midnight forest seemed to wrap them round in security. They lay down on a slope of grass below a willow thicket and for a little while their excited senses seemed still on the watch for danger, even after they had both dropped asleep.

But the silence all about lulled them into stupor beyond the dream of possible danger; for in the end they both slept in heavy exhaustion. Chris did not wake until a big hand took him by the shoulder and a voice spoke loudly almost in his ear. He sat up startled, to see the sun riding high above the trees and to take in the joyful knowledge that it was Eric Knudson who was stooping over him.

"I think I never find you," said Knudson, stirred out of his usual stolid manner and staring with wonder at the sight of a second youth where he had thought to discover only one.

Eric Knudson had an odd thing to tell, although he recounted it with little thought of what it meant to his two companions. He had rowed until almost morning, slept a little in the boat and then gone on with the first light. "I see a little cabin and thought you might have slept there, so I went up to it, leaving the boat, and pushed in the crazy door." He paused a moment contemplating even now his astonishment at what he discovered when that creaking door swung back.

"You saw two men?" Chris suggested, while Stuart, in the same breath, hazarded:

"There was no one there?"

"I saw one man," Eric Knudson corrected carefully, "and he was lying beside the fireplace because some one had struck him over the head. I wonder for a while what I should do, and whether this had anything to do with you. At last I see, far away over the trees, some smoke going up, which must mean a house. I walk a long way through the woods and tell the farmer there that down by the river there is a man lying, still breathing, and too big for me to carry all that way. Then I believe that I have done enough, so I come back to my boat and go on to look for you."

Chris stretched his arms asunder, and took a great relieved breath of the clean morning air. All that had passed might be put away now as of no more value than a dream; what was left was the knowledge that he had a comrade and the rest of the journey need not be so lonely. But a final thought flitted through his mind.

"Eric," he said, "did you happen to notice some lumps of stone, shiny yellow stone, lying on the hearth?" He felt somewhat like a little boy who has carelessly lost one of his marbles and wonders idly what has become of it.

Knudson reflected. "I did not see such a thing," he declared, "and I think I would have, for the man's head was lying on the hearth. A very big fellow he was. You say that there were two men there? They must have quarreled over something."

Of the lumps of fool gold, they never heard again.

Stuart Hale made some demur over what Chris took as a matter of course, that he was to go forward with them, share their supplies and see the adventure to its end. "You thought of it in the beginning," Chris insisted. "It would never have come about except for you."

"It would never have come about through me," said Stuart, "though it does look as though you could do with another hand. The drive is nearly at the end now and there aren't many miles to go. I wish I had been with it from the beginning."

The river had grown to a broad stream which Chris would scarcely have recognized to be the same waterway as the narrow rushing torrent upon whose waters they had set forth weeks ago. The current ran sluggishly and the logs drifted by, long and black, with their smooth bark gleaming where water and sun rippled over them alternately. With the unerring instinct of helpless things, however, even here they had found opportunity to make trouble, for a long row of them had nosed in to lie comfortably upon a mud flat under the overhanging bank. It was Stuart's idea, and a good one, that Chris should take the boat and row downstream to arrive among the first of the logs when they reached the mouth of the river.

"Knudson and I will stay behind to herd the stragglers," he said, "but some one must be there, to see that they are caught and do not run free into the Mississippi."

Chris embarked and rowed steadily mile after mile. He could see where acres of ground had been cut over for logs, which could readily be floated in the deep water to which he had come now. There were not many farms, only miles of jagged stumps with scrubby underbrush beginning to grow up between them. Rains had cut great gashes in the slopes, showing the naked clay where good black mould should have been. He realized that Grandfather had known what he was about when he had laid out so carefully the plan for the trees which they were to fell.

He traveled all day, with the logs all about and ahead of him, landed his boat, slept under it and fared on again. This seemed the longest part of the journey and the least pleasant; for he missed the excitement of the constant hazards and difficulties and he was disappointed that the companionship which was to come of Stuart's presence, must be so soon interrupted. But each phase of the work must be done and he rowed and rowed, past the green, unfamiliar shores, past certain of his own logs, floating slower but spread out in what seemed an interminable procession, past stretches of marsh and bits of yellow sandbar.

It was late afternoon when he finally came to the end of his pilgrimage. A freshening of the wind made him turn about to look, and he saw an opening in the trees before him and beyond it a broad gleam of water which reminded him of nothing other than Grandfather's tales of the sea. As he came nearer he could see that it was not quite the ocean, it was the Mississippi. The sea is not surrounded by woods, it does not move with slow majesty always in one certain direction. The sea, even under an overcast sky, never shows the smooth gleam of polished silver. But he dropped his oars and let the boat drift for the last quarter of a mile. A boy who has never seen a stream larger than the rushing Goose Wing, spanned by the toss of a stone from one hillside to another, does not soon forget his first sight of those vast waters whose valley drains a whole continent. Chris sat staring and drifting, and only after a long time was aware that he was coming to a green point, a row of cabins and a long curved boom, floating at the mouth of the Goose Wing River.

Gold in the Ashes

Several men stood along the shore, watching his approach, and one, a thickset fellow standing at the end of the boom, was catching the logs with an iron-shod pole and deftly bringing them in, one after another, to lie side by side along the shore. He spoke across the water as Chris and the boat came near.

"Where did this timber come from? It's a different quality of pine than what we cut hereabouts. And it's marked with a stamp we've never seen. Looks like the outline of a tree!"

"It came from the head of Goose Wing River, just below the Range," Chris told him and saw the man's face lengthen in wonder.

"Nobody's ever tried to drive logs so far as that before," he marveled. "Whose are they?" After a moment of staring at the boy before him, a boy with blond, sunburned hair, tired eyes and a gleaming smile, he inquired in further astonishment, "Yours?"

Chris nodded. He was suddenly conscious that his arms ached with the long unaccustomed rowing and that, in these unfamiliar surroundings, he had no idea what to do or to say next. He watched the easy skill with which the other swung the logs to shore by one motion of his iron-hooked pole. It seemed to him an impossible thing that two people like himself and Eric Knudson, clumsy and with no experience, should set out on such a task as driving logs a hundred miles or more down a shallow river. He wondered dazedly how they had come to reach their journey's end. The big walnut log, with its spruce outriggers, came floating down among the others, shouldering the lesser timbers aside and sliding wearily toward a place of rest beside the bank. The broad man's eyes opened wide with amazed admiration.

"Whoever you are, you're a born logger if you can bring a piece of timber like that down from the hill country. It looks like Noah's Ark amongst a school of minnows." He stood in silent marveling as the trunk of the little nut tree rolled over in the gentle current before it finally came to shore and lay still. Then he turned to Chris once more.

"You had better go up and make a dicker with Shreve McCloud. He's a straight man and he'll treat you right. You'll want to do one of two things, sell these now, or raft them down the Mississippi. You couldn't do better business than to let these logs go down river with his pilot." He regarded Chris carefully for a whole minute. "Pierre Dumenille might like you, though he doesn't like many. He might take you with him."

CHAPTER IV

MARCHING WATERS

A slab shanty beside the long row of log cribs did duty for an office. It was the place of business of that Company which, for several years, had been cutting and rafting logs from the banks of the Mississippi and of the deep, final reach of the Goose Wing. As Chris opened the door and stood for a minute upon the threshold, he saw two men sitting on opposite sides of the rough table. One of them was just getting up to go, rising from his stool with that smooth motion of lithe muscles which made the boy think, suddenly and involuntarily:

"Why, what is an Indian doing here?"

In spite of his big boots, his Mackinaw coat and his close-cropped hair, he was undoubtedly a red man. When he turned round, however, he showed a familiar countenance and a smile of recognition. Of course, Chris recollected, this was Pierre Dumenille, towering above him with his dark head almost touching the axe-hewn rafters of the little building. How good it was to see a face upon which he had laid eyes even once before. He felt almost as though the half-Chippewa pilot were an old friend. Dumenille was speaking to his comrade, whose Scotch ruddiness marked him unmistakably as Shreve McCloud.

"Here at last is the fellow who belongs to those logs which have been drifting in from day to day, and about which we have had so much talk and wonder."

It took no long discussion to settle what was to be the next fortune of the log flotilla. There was, as the man outside had made clear, no chance to doubt the hearty honesty of Shreve McCloud. He told the boy frankly that the lumber would be sold to better advantage if it were carried together to St. Louis.

"I have a shipbuilding friend who comes up from New Orleans to buy timber; he is an excitable fellow who would weep upon the shoulder of a man who will bring him walnut. Can you really tell me that you have floated hardwood logs all this way?"

Chris pointed out to him, through the window, the scattered walnut logs showing conspicuously amongst the straight black timbers of white pine. The main trunk of Grandfather's nut tree loomed enormous above the others. McCloud shook his head in marveling that it should ever have sailed to the end of such a voyage.

Marching Waters

"It must have caught on the rapids a hundred times," he observed, and Chris assured him that it was even so. Over and over again he and Knudson had stood waist deep in water, pushing and dragging at a wildly tumbled heap of logs reaching high above their heads, with always the huge mass of Grandfather's nut tree at the vital point of the jam.

"It might be better," said the Scotchman thoughtfully, "to sledge such hardwood lumber all the way down the valley while the snow still holds. We will see when the timber comes to market whether the walnut brings enough to make such a long haul worth while. I will arrange to sell it for you to the special man who wants it most. And for the pine, it was a famous way to bring it down from the hills, though it needed a bold heart to try such a thing."

"I — I would like to go to St. Louis with it," Chris declared. He knew nothing of rafting, nothing of the long river, or the busy frontier city of St. Louis where his market must lie. But he felt that he must see this venture to its final end. After one further look at Pierre Dumenille, he knew his desire to be increased a hundred-fold. There was a French charm about this man of boldly erect Indian build, a warming quality in his smile, which laid instant hold of something very deep within a shy and lonely boy.

McCloud looked doubtful over Chris Dahlberg's request and glanced across at his pilot.

"Will you take him as a raft hand?" he asked. "We don't carry passengers when we float our brails down river."

Chris felt these sharp, black eyes examining him keenly. He seemed to himself unbelievably clumsy and awkward under that rapid scrutiny, no fit material for work which requires experience and skill. But Pierre Dumenille put only one question:

"Of what was it you were speaking, that day that we met in the snow? Was something said of — was it of a grandfather back yonder in the valley?" As Chris nodded, the pilot turned to McCloud. "I take him," he declared briefly, and his face lit, as the boy's did also, with a flash of pleasure.

Chris Dahlberg was to learn that this man carried within him the Indian instinct for rocks and waters and furiously running channels which is only bred in long generations of forest voyagers. When this is combined with the power to handle men and to bring them to act under his bidding, there is made such a pilot as the river seldom sees. He was, beyond all other men, a master of swift water.

For days the logs came leisurely to port and at last, at the end of the long procession, arrived Eric Knudson and Stuart. Already preparations were under way for the voyage downstream. There were not enough of the Goose Wing River timbers to make so big a raft as Pierre Dumenille was accustomed to navigate; but with the logs which McCloud had on hand, the proper size would be completed. These and Chris Dahlberg's would make up three strips, or brails as he was taught to call them, and were a quite sufficient number to be worth carrying together to the market. Knudson was to return to his farm, since he showed no inclination for the new experience of a voyage down the Mississippi. Shreve McCloud bought, on the spot, enough of the white pine to make it possible for Chris to pay Knudson a sufficient wage for his labors. He set off next morning on the long tramp homeward, carrying a letter from Chris to Alexis Dahlberg.

"Anna and I, we will take good care of your grandfather until you come back," he assured the boy. "You should be with us before winter; we will do well enough until the snows come."

Shreve McCloud, being short of helpers, offered Stuart Hale temporary employment, which the lad was glad to accept. He threw himself into the work of sorting logs and helping with the building of the raft with just the enthusiasm he always seemed to have for a new enterprise. The men all liked him, for he was quick to learn what to do, and showed no disposition to shirk his full measure of the work. Far more rapidly than Chris, he became well acquainted with all their laboring companions.

One morning, when a sudden squall of wind and rain had interrupted their activities, the whole company sat under the shelter of an open shed waiting until they could resume their work. Pierre Dumenille and one or two others were talking together, discussing the different pilots whom they had known, and comparing their skill in navigating keel boats, rafts, and the very few steamboats which at that time had found their way to the upper Mississippi. They named one and another, enumerating their merits and their failings. At a little pause in the talk, Stuart joined in easily:

"I came up the river on a keel boat and I sailed with a man who must have been as good as any of these you have been talking about. While you are speaking of pilots, why does nobody mention as good a one as Joe Langford?"

At his words, Pierre Dumenille spun about in his seat to face the boy with a very blaze of wrath upon his dark countenance. He seemed about to pour forth a flood of anger upon his questioner that would fairly

Marching Waters

drown him. But instead he checked himself abruptly, rose, and walked away through the group of men. The rain ceased; the work was taken up again; but Pierre Dumenille did not come back.

Stuart, astonished and uncomfortable, sought enlightenment from Jacob Woolf, the thickset man whom Chris had first seen collecting logs inside the boom.

"What was the matter?" Stuart asked. "Why had Dumenille any right to behave so over what I said?"

"That is a bad business," Woolf expounded to the two boys. "Langford and Dumenille were cub pilots together and were the best friends in the world. Then they quarreled. They were both pilots for Shreve Mc-Cloud; they are still for that matter, though they never see each other. There was a time when they were taking a raft down together, and making a stormy run of it so that not a man had a chance for rest, day or night. By the third morning Langford was staggering for want of sleep. Pierre is like a cat; he seems to have no need for sleeping when there is danger abroad. Dumenille came out to relieve his friend and found him fairly asleep on his legs; hardly any man could have helped it after what they had all been through. There was a reef ahead and the raft just swinging into it, when Pierre caught the steering

115

sweep out of Langford's hand. He saved the raft, but Joe Langford flashed out on him in a perfect fury of resentment. Nobody really will ever know what was said between them; but now people can't mention Langford's name where Pierre Dumenille is. It wasn't a thing one pilot does to another; but there was no time to speak, not even for a fellow as quick as Pierre. Langford never got over it."

Stuart took the misfortune of his awkward speech in very bad part. "He had no right to turn on me like that," he declared indignantly and more than once to Chris. It was plain that he felt unhappy over the mischance; but his unhappiness and mortification he attempted to conceal under an outward show of irritation. Pierre Dumenille came back to the work next day with a face which betrayed no memory of what had passed; but it was quite evident, thereafter, that he and Stuart avoided each other's company.

Some days later, when Chris urged that Stuart apply to go down the river with the rafting venture, his friend would have nothing to do with the idea. "I don't mind working my way," he burst out, "but I won't have a Chippewa half-breed giving me orders." And to this opinion he clung obstinately.

To Chris it was the most interesting thing in the world to see the hands of practised laborers assembling the raft. Long logs were bolted together, end to end, by means of huge wooden pins and short chains of three links. A great frame made up of these bolted logs floated on the water; while inside floated the smaller logs, not fastened together, but laid in rows and sorted as to size. This ungainly, flexible structure was braced and stiffened by the erection of snubbing posts, and the laying and stretching of diagonal raft lines, long ropes which held the gigantic framework firm. When one brail, or section, was completed, it was floated down near to the mouth of the Goose Wing River to wait for the rest.

Even so early in these experimental days of logging, a few steamboats were available to take rafts to their destination. Shreve McCloud, however, employed the slower and cheaper method of floating. Tremendous sweeps, like oars, were mounted in blocks at the bow and stern of each section, running fore and aft. With these the raftsmen could row the ends in one direction or another and, under the orders of a skilful pilot like Dumenille, could steer the unwieldy craft through all the difficulties of reefs and rapids.

The morning came when the voyagers were to launch out into the Mississippi. Rude platforms and wooden sheds had been built upon the rafts, for the men to sleep in and for the storage of provisions. As each of the crew was being assigned to his place, one big Canadian broke into raging protest over some task which Pierre Dumenille had laid upon him. The tall pilot, who was walking away after delivering his order, turned about and looked at the fellow slowly from head to heel. The stream of angry words faltered and grew thin; the man choked, hesitated and suddenly turned about to do the other's bidding. Jacob Woolf, who was to go, stood beside Chris and said in grinning satisfaction:

"A good pilot has to be big enough to knock down any man of his crew that disagrees with him. But Dumenille doesn't often need to do it."

The expedition was to start at daybreak, but it was still cool twilight when Chris arose and gathered his small possessions into a bundle. He stood for a moment looking down at Stuart Hale who lay stretched across his bunk still in deep slumber. The older boy's white face had grown brown, and the hollows in his cheeks had filled; but there was still a furrow of discontented wrinkles between his eyebrows which even the peace of slumber had not smoothed away. A strange fellow he was, never satisfied, always craving for something new.

This was the first near friend that Chris had ever

known, some one of his own age who felt things in somewhat the same way that he did, who looked out upon the vague promises of the future with something of the same wonder. They were to be parted now, possibly with no chance of meeting again. It would be easier to endure the wrench without attempting any words of good-bye. Chris stole away, leaving Stuart still asleep, and went out into the gray morning.

The raft lay rocking on the current beside the long boom. Dumenille's great figure stood at the end of the slip to see the last supplies taken on board. Very conscious of being the most untried member of the crew, Chris walked slowly along the runway of floating logs to embark. Suddenly he heard hasty feet behind and an excited voice calling to him. Stuart Hale, breathless, came up beside him.

"Chris, what a fool I have been! I want to go with you."

Both the boys looked up in desperate anxiety to search the dark face of Pierre Dumenille. As he turned slowly about to look at them, a deliberate grin spread across his countenance. It seemed as though he understood the whole situation. Though his smile was slow, his decision was immediate.

"If he can walk to the end of the raft and back

without getting wet, I will take him and leave that ill-tempered one behind." He jerked his head toward the fellow who had disputed his orders the day before.

Stuart, without an instant of hesitation, jumped from the boom to the floating stringpiece of the huge craft. There is no small art in walking upon a raft, where the logs float free and where each one ducks under water when the weight of a man's foot rests upon it for more than an instant. It is only possible to make progress by stepping so rapidly from one log to another that there is no time to sink. The raft was a big one, but Stuart moved the length of it with a speed and lightness which not even Pierre himself could have equaled. He reached the far end and came swiftly back, his face all alight with excitement and pleasure. Pierre Dumenille laughed aloud as the boy stepped upon the boom. The logs over which Stuart had traveled were wet from their ducking, but his boots were dry.

"You shall go. Get ashore, Antoine, you are to stay behind this time."

The pilot's order is law and not even Shreve McCloud would have protested against his decision. The Canadian, muttering and fuming, disembarked as he **was** bid, and Stuart and Chris stepped on board. The lines were cast off, the raft was headed into the current and floated easily away.

Chris looked back as they came through the mouth of the river and slid into the wide reach of the Mississippi. It was full daylight now, one of those clear summer mornings on which it seems that one can see for an infinite number of miles. It would be hot later. The sky was pale, and the pale, creamy clouds, piled high and rolling, were scarcely distinguishable against the faint blue. The boy could see afar, up a great length of the course of the Goose Wing River to where the green hills began to rise and to the faint distant looming of the higher range within whose folds lay his own valley. He had a strange sense of there being something very great and portentous in their slow progress out from the smaller river into the greater. And yet the raft was a mere dot in that wide landscape and he himself the tiniest of figures standing at the stern.

The voyage of a raft has long monotonous stretches interspersed with moments of sharp danger. It is a frail craft at best, laid flat upon the water and undulating from end to end, apparently with no more substance than a sheet of paper. It is usually four hundred feet long, more than the length of a modern city block and, with the brails laid side by side, nearly half

Swift Rivers

as wide. A furious wind can rock and toss the logs
until, occasionally, they wash out of their floating
framework and are scattered over the river. There
are long chains of rapids where it has happened to
more than one pilot, sliding downward with the angry
water, to run afoul of a sharp reef and rip his craft
from end to end, sending the logs swirling over the
face of the whole stream, perhaps never to be gathered again.

Con O'Blennes, the genial cook, said to Stuart and
Chris: "It is a job to break your heart, trying to get a
raft together, once it's been broken up. Every man on
the river wants to ship with a good pilot who won't
get his crew into such a jam. They all try their best to
get work under Pierre Dumenille." He added in a
whisper, "Or with Joe Langford."

Dumenille was not to take the logs all the way to
St. Louis, it was revealed. Canny Shreve McCloud,
making the most of his two good pilots who would
not meet, used Pierre for the most part on the upper
reach of the voyage and let Langford take over the
task for the last half of the way. Joe Langford was
ahead of them now, setting out from Prairie du
Chien for the first run of the season. Later he would
take command after Dumenille had brought them below the great barrier of the first rapids.

Marching Waters

Not only did the valley of the great stream wind southward with never a straight mile anywhere, but also the current and the channel went back and forth between the banks with an infinity of twists and turns. This channel every floating craft must follow, even though the shallow draft of a raft gave it a little more freedom than had the deeper keel boats. Each passage from shore to shore was called a crossing; and only by knowing the crossings and all their shifts and changes could a man steer safely the craft under his charge.

"Lone Tree Crossing is the worst place on the river," Con O'Blennes informed the two. "Wherever you see rivermen talking together, you know they may be arguing whether the rapids at Rock Island or the rapids opposite the mouth of the Des Moines River are the worst; but they'll all be agreeing that they don't dread rapids as they do the Lone Tree Bar. Pierre will carry us over the first rapids, but it's Langford who'll be steering us when we come to Lone Tree Crossing. There's no pilot or crew breathes easy until they're clear of it."

Pierre Dumenille had taken Chris with him as oarsman one day when they went ashore in the raft boat, a shallow-water cousin to the Atlantic coast dory. They landed at a handful of houses which hopeful persons

might have called a town and where a little store contained frontier supplies laboriously freighted up the
river. They bought food and quinine from a small,
whining man, perpetually complaining of the bad
times. His wife was a comely woman with a tired,
sensible face. She packed up the purchases which
Pierre had made and, while doing so, held a whispered colloquy with her husband in a corner. The
man, unwilling to do something which his wife was
urging, presently raised his voice in alarmed remon-
strance:

"You'll get us into trouble, Deborah, if you go talking about things you've no business to."

Deborah, however, driven evidently by conscience,
was not to be silenced. Since her husband would not
speak, she came forward to address Pierre Dumenille
herself:

"There was a raft passed down last week, the first
that came this season, starting from Prairie du Chien.
Isn't that a hundred miles below the Goose Wing?
Her pilot was — was once a friend of yours, Pierre."

It required a braver person than the little store-
keeper to face the hard stare which Pierre Dumenille
bent upon her. But with the persistence of a woman
following her sense of right, Deborah went on deter-
minedly:

Marching Waters

"Joe Langford was sick, dreadfully sick, when they brought the raft inshore and asked if they could carry him up to our place to lie in a bed for a few days. I did what I could for him, but he was in one of those wasting fevers that just go through with their course and no one can stop them. He was out of his head, or they wouldn't have been able to get him to leave his raft; he lay here raving for three nights and he kept calling for you, Pierre, for you, all the time. He got a little better, finally, and there was no keeping him here once he could leave his bed. He looked to me like a man sick to death, but he would go on. I — I was certain you ought to know, Pierre Dumenille, though I know you don't thank me for telling you."

Dumenille's French politeness did not allow him to be rude to a lady, even though she was a backwoodsman's wife in a linsey-woolsey dress and a denim apron. "You have done what you thought you ought to," he said to her in a tone which held no hint of expression, "but now that your duty is performed, we need say no more." Without a backward glance, he walked out of the store and made his way to the boat lying on the shore.

He did not speak for some time but finally, when they were half way back to the raft, he made some observation to Chris in his ordinary voice, and from that time on talked to him of water and currents and all the small matters of life on the river. Neither then nor later did he make reference to what the conscientious Deborah had said to him.

Although Chris Dahlberg was, technically, the owner of a large portion of the logs which they were carrying southward with such care, not one of the crew treated him other than as a raft hand, a young and inexperienced one who had much to learn. The men were an odd assortment of husky fellows who seemed to have but one thing in common, a coarseness and hardness beyond anything which Chris had ever dreamed of. Their toiling, comfortless life appeared to have made of their minds and hearts a barren waste. From their talk it was to be gathered that their only thoughts were concerned with the end of the voyage and the joys of flinging their wages broadcast in a brief space of glorious freedom before they were penniless and must set to work again. They talked much, all of them, of the one or two stopping places which their course afforded. The two stretches of rapids could only be passed under proper conditions of weather and water.

"We always tie up for a bit when we get to the Rock Island Rapids, to wait for the wind to be right," Jacob Woolf told the two boys. "And the Des Moines

Marching Waters

Rapids, too, might hold us up for a while at Montrose. That's the time when a man can look forward to a little pleasure ashore."

Chris wondered often whether Stuart Hale would endure for long a state of things which seemed exactly calculated to arouse his fretting impatience. Dumenille ruled with iron discipline; his orders were quick and must be instantly obeyed. The work was heavy; the food was coarse; there were days when the blaze of the sun above and the reflected glare from the water made the heat almost unbearable. The crossed raft lines which held the whole structure in its proper shape were prone to stretch, so that there was constant labor at winding the heavy windlasses to keep them taut.

There was no real dullness, however, in a journey which was always on the point of turning a corner into a new scene of adventure amongst the islands and sandbars. And the evenings and the summer nights made up for anything which the day might bring. The sun would go down in crimson majesty behind the green bluffs; the cool dark would come with a soft breeze to creep over the water and fan hot, burned faces. The canopy of stars would hang splendidly overhead, with a rippling pattern of their brightness reflected in the water below. The voice of

the river, never so audible by day, could be heard deep
and commanding, as the huge body of water, carrying
the tiny speck of the raft along with it, went marching
past the silent forest in never-resting pilgrimage.
Stuart and Chris, lying side by side with their faces
to the sky, would talk in whispers, while their comrades sprawled in ungainly attitudes of slumber all
about them. Pierre Dumenille seemed, indeed, to re-
quire only half the amount of slumber that another
man would take. Chris always thought of him, afterward, as he used to see him on those soft June
nights, standing erect in the stern, with his eyes fixed
far away, a magnificent, bronze statue against the
stars.

As their journey progressed, some of the boats
which they met would lie alongside for a little, to exchange talk and tobacco, and to compare notes on the
upper and the lower portions of the channel. The
boys began to hear more and more of that next hazard
which they were to pass, the chain of rapids at the foot
of which lay the big Rock Island. Pierre Dumenille
asked anxiously of every man with whom he could
get speech, what was the stage of water on the Rock
Island reefs. It was going down, each one told him.
As the reports gave it as falling lower and lower, the
pilot's face became increasingly troubled.

Marching Waters

The last man with whom they spoke, a trader paddling a canoe northward, gave the most discouraging report of all. "This raft of yours makes four that's started from places on the Mississippi south of the Goose Wing and gone down this season. Only one got over the rapids, the two that followed don't dare run farther and are tied up at the banks above Rock Island. The men are all waiting, idle, for a rain to come."

Chris had an opportunity to speak to him in an undertone just before he cast loose. "Was one of those rafts that are waiting — was one Joe Langford's?"

The trader shot a cautious glance all about lest Pierre overhear. All the river, it seemed, knew what it was to speak that name in Dumenille's presence.

"No," he replied for Chris alone, "Joe's was the first raft and he went over. They say he was sick, but wouldn't give up, for all his men could say to him. I met him just as he was swinging out into the rapids and I am sure he got past them safe. He and Pierre are the only two who would have dared such a thing in this low water."

It was the next day that the voyagers dropped round the final bend and came within sight of the rapids at last. At the foot of them, long and low, lay a great island with shores of white stone. The smoke of an

Indian village went up from a green headland on the eastern shore; but on the west bank were white men's cabins and a lengthy building of logs set a hundred yards from the water's edge. Two rafts, both smaller than theirs, lay moored to the bank.

As they came nearer, Chris could see breaks and riffles in the water, showing where the sharp reefs stretched below the surface. Some of the rocks lay bare and dry in the hot sun, their jagged outline giving hint of what dangers were hidden just beneath the water. It was not a stretch of tumbling foam and whirlpools, as rapids are in a smaller stream. The Mississippi is too big for that. It was a faintly discernible slope, many miles long, broken and crisscrossed and interlaced with sinister dark streaks where a huge, rushing current fell from pool to pool over sharp-edged barriers of upturned rocks.

"The old Mississipp' is showing her teeth," commented Con O'Blennes. There was running and shouting and the splash of the sweeps in the water, for the raft was to come to land for the first time since they had set out.

The men were wild to get ashore. All along the bank were loud calls of greeting from friends on the other rafts whose crews were waiting in noisy idleness for the water to rise. Pierre Dumenille, however, kept all of his men busy, tightening up lines and warping the great craft into exactly the right mooring; so that it was evening before they were free. For once they were unexcited by the announcement, "Grub pile," and could scarcely wait to bolt the supper which Con set before them. The goal of their anticipation was the long building which bore the ominously hospitable sign, "Mike Shannon's Place. Come in."

Stuart and Chris were also looking forward to the opportunity of stretching their legs on dry land once more. There were a few last duties still to be performed, however, and these they stayed to finish while the rest of the crew went hurrying over the side and scrambling up the bank. But Con O'Blennes, clearing up after the hasty supper, spoke to the boys in friendly warning:

"If I was you, I wouldn't go ashore to-night," he advised. "A place like this, with a gang of idle rafting crews in it, makes about the toughest spot you could ever hope to find. There's many a one who wasn't on to the ways of things that's been found in the morning with a split head and his pockets empty. Not that they're really a bad lot," he made haste to explain, "but it's just that they fall out with strangers when they're drinking and excited like."

Chris was willing enough to wait until morning;

for the day had been intensely hot and the quiet of the raft was pleasant after the bustle of making land. Stuart was more reluctant to remain on board; but when they both saw that Pierre Dumenille was making no move to seek the pleasures of the town, he also was willing to stay. Con O'Blennes went whistling about his work. It was plain that he was a peaceable man and had no craving for the excitements that drew the others.

Pierre Dumenille sat staring moodily at the vast passing waters. Chris knew that he was anxious. Rafts must not stay in the water too long, for the wood gets waterlogged in time, and some of the largest trunks sink and are lost. It was a long voyage from Goose Wing River and they would not fare the better for this delay.

The air was still very quiet and very hot. A great storm cloud was passing around to the north of them, towering high in the empty sky. The flashes of lightning could be seen between its peaks; the rumble of the thunder was low and distant; and a curtain of rain trailed below it.

"I wish it would pass over us," Chris thought. He could hear the din of roaring voices and of great bursts of boisterous laughter from Mike Shannon's Place. It was pleasanter to listen to the cool swish of

the water among the logs instead. Presently he heard
Con O'Blennes speak from his place under the cooking shelter:

"There must have been big rain up above, Cap. The
water's coming up."

"Yes," Pierre Dumenille nodded. "I have been
watching it. And there is also going to be wind in a
minute."

Yet even he had not augured what the wind would
be. It swooped down upon them with a sudden scream,
lashing the river and tossing the rafts like chips where
they lay along the shore. Chris could hear the shouts
of the watchmen left in charge of the other rafts, as
they ran hurrying up and down to make things fast.
Pierre Dumenille was the first man to lay hand upon
a line. His voice never lifted beyond the exact need
for making his orders heard; but his commands flew
as the four of them scurried about. The raft wavered
and tossed on the long billows which ran under its
limber framework from end to end. The rain followed
in driving fury, blotting out the faint light of the fading day and bringing black night upon them with a
rush. Through the noise Chris heard Pierre Dumenille
speak close to him:

"The water has lifted; I am going to take the raft
down the rapids."

"When?" asked Chris astonished. "Now, in the dark? And how about the men?"

Con O'Blennes, overhearing, spoke in pleading protest:

"In the dark and the rain, sir? And the men having their first time ashore! They won't one of them be willing to come."

But Pierre's decision was made. "The water may fall again by morning. We are going over to-night. I need Stuart to help me wind the cross lines and stiffen her up. He's the quickest one to run over logs in the dark. You stay here and hold this sweep steady for your life, Con, to keep her head against the shore. Chris," he hesitated, but in an instant went on. "I don't like much to send you, Chris, but I can't leave the raft and Con would be no good. You will have to go up yonder and fetch the men."

There could never have been a heavier task laid upon Chris than such an errand as this. What power could a boy, used to the solitudes of the forests, manage to exert over a crowd of surly and unwilling raft hands? Yet he could not hang back when Pierre Dumenille had sent him. He jumped from the edge of the raft and, even as he did so, saw Pierre and Stuart running to set their shoulders against the windlass. The water heaved and lapped against the bank, to make strange gurgles and sucking noises amongst the chafing logs. Chris scrambled up the steep path to the level of the shore above him.

The little log houses were all silent and without a light as he threaded his way amongst them; although before him, at the end of the semblance of a street, the long building of Mike Shannon's Place showed every window blazing and the yellow light streaming out around the cracks of the clumsily fitting door. Chris walked up the pathway, where choking dust had been changed, in the last few minutes, into slippery mud, past dooryards where the earth was trodden bare or where at best the straggling weeds flourished tall and untidily abundant. He thought, for some reason, of the high meadow with its clean sweet air, with the scent of pine trees and the fragrance of ripe berries with the sun upon them. He thought of Grandfather and of how the old man's eyes would have danced with joyous excitement over just such an adventure which Chris was facing. Many a time, in the strange ports of the world, Grandfather must have gone forth to fetch a reluctant and rebellious crew to put to sea again. Chris would have a tale to match Grandfather's, if he could only bring this undertaking to a successful end. He laid his hand steadily on the big wooden latch, opened the door and went in.

Swift Rivers

There were two rooms in the space inside; so that he could see the bar with its lights and its clinking tin cups beyond an inner door. The low-roofed place was lit by smoking oil lamps and was crowded from wall to wall with men who looked, in that red light, to be all alike. They were all long-limbed, heavy, and roughly dressed. He did distinguish Jacob Woolf on a bench close to the wall, but the other faces seemed only like some strange pattern of lowering brows and curious eyes as one and all turned to look at him. A great draft of hot, close air poured past him to the open door.

Some of the men were gambling at the rough tables, more were sprawled idly on the long benches. All of them had been drinking; and in the sudden silence which fell at sight of him, a dozen more came crowding through the door from the bar.

He hardly knew his own voice when he spoke. He had been afraid that it might shake with excitement, but it came forth steady and peremptory. "Pierre Dumenille has sent for his crew. He is going to run the rapids to-night."

A long man in the corner, whom Chris had never seen before, one of the crew of a waiting raft, ripped out a big, rolling exclamation of surprise and reluctant admiration. "Pierre Dumenille is a bold man to try such a thing as that. There's fifty chances to one that he'll split on the rocks and the river will get his logs. And what the Mississippi takes, she doesn't willingly give back again."

But his was the only voice to speak aloud. The rest of that company sat for another minute in sullen silence which broke presently into angry mutterings. Another man, one of their own crew, spoke at last:

"Pierre Dumenille is a fool, and I ride no rapids in the dark with him. Go back and tell him so."

A great roar of laughter went up. Chris thought, for an instant, that he must fall back before it; then he felt indignation burn hot in his heart. An amazing lust for battle, such as his quiet nature had never known before, flamed up within him. He felt a little as he had when he had faced Uncle Nels' bellowing rage. Here were fifty of Uncle Nels' kind, angry, resisting, totally against him. In his throbbing excitement he was not afraid of one or of all of them. He stepped forward into the middle of the room. He could not know how thin and slight he looked in the midst of that crowd of burly giants. Nor could he know how his face had lit with a sudden intensity of confidence and power.

"Jacob Woolf," he said steadily, "get up from your bench and go about your work."

Swift Rivers

A raftsman lives by orders; he does not hire out his brains, but falls into the habit of thinking little and doing what he is told. From pure force of long custom, Jacob Woolf heeded the sharp order and shambled to the door.

"So long, fellows," he observed grinning, "I reckon I'll give Pierre Dumenille a run for his money after all."

One by one Chris picked out his own men by name and ordered them out. If he had been surprised at their obeying, the battle would have been lost; but not even he had the least thought that they would hesitate. One by one they got up in deliberate response, and followed Jacob Woolf through the door. The last one was just stepping over the threshold and Chris was turning to follow when a big man with a low forehead and bristling, red hair strode suddenly in his way. Amid every company there is always an arch trouble maker, and this was he.

"There's no bully on the river like Pierre Dumenille," he said in a huge voice which filled the whole room. "A man's a simpleton to take orders from him, whether he brings them himself or sends another where he doesn't dare to come." A shout of applause greeted this statement and then dropped suddenly to hear what Chris might say. He had turned upon the threshold to reply:

"Pierre Dumenille sent me to get his own men, not to hire extra hands. He'll run the rapids to-night without need of any help from you."

A wave of derisive laughter fairly rocked the crowded room. Chris went out and closed the door after him, taking a deep breath of the wet night air. His men were vaguely visible in the dark making their way in sullen silence down the crooked street. Jacob Woolf fell back to walk beside him.

"You handled them good," he volunteered. "I didn't think any one of them would come." He concluded in surprised candor, "I didn't think I would come myself. And that was well, how you put it to Spike Ellerby. He's a man that sets trouble going wherever he is. He shipped with Pierre Dumenille two seasons ago. Pierre ordered him off at Prairie du Chien, and there's been bad blood between them ever since."

The other men offered no word but went splashing through the wet, stumbled down the slippery bank and went silently on board the raft. Dumenille's low-pitched orders assigned each one to his work as he appeared out of the darkness. It seemed as though they were about to set forward peaceably, but it was not to be. There was suddenly a sound of trampling feet and loud voices on the bank, while the flash of lanterns showed that a portion of the company from the building above had come trooping down to the shore. Most of them stood in a huddle at the top of the bank, but a half dozen with Spike Ellerby came down the steep incline and stood at the edge of the water.

"Pierre Dumenille," Spike Ellerby's big voice summoned the pilot through the dark, "you've no right to take men into danger for the sake of a few logs. If that crew of yours has a spark of spirit amongst them, they'll come ashore and leave you." He raised his voice higher and called, "Baines, Harris, was it you who were boasting up at Mike's that no Injun pilot could drive you where you didn't want to go?"

The two men whom he had called dropped their work and came doubtfully to the edge of the raft. "You're right," said one of them suddenly, "I'll stand by what I said." He jumped to shore in the dark. As many as nine or ten more stood in an uncertain group along the boom piece, not quite decided what they should do.

Pierre Dumenille moved from the place where he had been standing in silence and picked up a lantern. He spoke softly, but Chris felt a chill run through him in the hot blackness as he heard the cold, completely controlled fury in the pilot's voice. Indians are good haters; and all the generations of Chippewa blood were speaking through Pierre Dumenille's voice in the dark:

"Come up here, Spike Ellerby. There is a thing which you and I will settle before I set out to-night."

Ellerby, in a loud bluster of incoherent abuse, might have hesitated, but his comrades thrust him forward. He stepped heavily upon the edge of the raft, trod the logs between with easy skill, and came upon the rude platform at the stern. He was breathing rapidly, while Dumenille still stood at his ease beside one of the long sweeps.

"Bring a torch, Chris," the pilot directed. "No man shall say that we did not give this Ellerby a fair chance."

A torch was an iron basket full of pine splinters suspended at the end of a short iron pole. When it was to be used, it was thrust into a slanted socket at the edge of the raft so that it hung out over the water. If fragments of burning wood fell from it, they dropped with a harmless hiss into the black depths. Chris set it alight and watched it burn furiously, shedding a red glare over every face and form within its flickering reach. Con O'Blennes came to help him; but Chris could see that his hands were trembling and could hear his breath coming in little sobbing gasps.

"Spike Ellerby is the most dangerous man on the river," he whispered to Chris. "I don't know what's to become of us, I don't know what's to become of us!"

Chris looked up at those two black figures moving warily into their places within the ring of crimson light. He realized that Stuart had come up beside him and was saying in his ear: "Stand by to get to Dumenille if the fellow knocks him out. Those men ashore will rush him the minute he goes under."

Chris was watching, fascinated, as he saw the two shuffle a little on the rough floor, each one feeling for a spot of certain footing. He thought he wanted to close his eyes, but instead found them staring, wide open. He saw Dumenille drawing himself together and knew that the desperate instant was coming.

Probably Spike Ellerby never really understood just what it was that knocked him overboard. His sledge hammer blow was reputed to be quick, but it was a thing of leisurely awkwardness compared with the lightning speed of the Chippewa Frenchman. There was a great splash, a shout of consternation and anger from the spectators on shore, and then Pierre Dumenille's orders coming like pistol shots through the darkness:

Marching Waters

"Get ashore, you, Baines and Harris, both of you that's been standing there gaping. I'll not have a man on board who goes following like a sheep after such talk as Ellerby's. Yes, I mean you, and you. Off with you. I'll run the rapids if I do it sole alone."

Indecision still seemed to weigh upon the minds of those who had harkened to Ellerby's counsel. But there was no doubting the determination of Pierre Dumenille and, as they saw Spike Ellerby, brought limp and dripping out of the shallow ripples, they seemed to feel a simultaneous urge to avoid a similar fate. The second man disembarked in headlong haste, splashing through the water in his speed of departure.

"How will you ever get over the rapids short-handed?" Con O'Blennes asked Dumenille. "Will you double trip her?"

The pilot answered briefly. "Yes, that is what I would have had to do anyway. I have two hands worth a dozen of that pair we are rid of."

Double tripping consisted in dividing the raft into sections and carrying them over the rapids one after another. Dumenille gave swift directions as to what was to be done, and by means of rapid effort, the crew had presently divided the outer strip from the rest and floated it free. Con O'Blennes and two others were to remain to see to the safety of the second por-

143

tion, while Pierre, the two boys, Jacob Woolf, and the others were to make the passage of the rapids. In the flurry of preparation, Stuart had disappeared for a few minutes, but presently emerged from the dark to pull a line beside Chris.

"I was tying up Ellerby's head," he explained, in the intervals of their heaving on the rope. "Pierre lifted up the torch and saw me doing it, but he didn't say a word."

The rain had swept past; the clouds were breaking and the moon was sailing clear as they drifted out and felt the strong hand of the current laid upon them.

CHAPTER V

THE KING OF SPAIN'S DAUGHTER

As the long raft came out into the moonlit channel, Jacob Woolf, standing beside Chris, spoke hoarsely:

"It must have been a big downpour up yonder, for the river is coming up steadily. Luck goes with such a man as Pierre Dumenille."

The white light illuminated, with almost uncanny brilliance, the long stretch of broken water before them. The riffles sang in the soft wind. What Chris knew to be lines of reefs were now only black marks upon a sheet of silver.

"How long are the rapids?" he asked Jacob Woolf, and received the answer ·

"Fifteen miles. The worst part is about the middle."

No more was said, for, in the clearness of the night, Chris could see the forward part of the long raft slide over into the incline of the river's downward sweep. There was silence no longer since the loud water was all about them and Pierre Dumenille's voice went ringing down the length of the tremendous, ungainly craft.

145

Swift Rivers

It seemed to Chris that he had scarcely time to breathe, far less to think, during that crowded time in which they made the passage of those fateful fifteen miles. He turned into a mere machine which rowed his long sweep backward and forward in instant response to sharp command. One upthrusting of black rocks was so close to where Chris stood that he could have stepped out upon it dry-shod. He pulled for his very life and was conscious that Pierre Dumenille's tremendous grasp was on the handgrip above his own and was rowing with him. The corner of the raft swung free with scarcely an inch of margin; they floated downward through a pool and came into another chain of reefs. In the curve of the current the immense craft curved also and swung this way and that; it ceased to be ungainly and was almost as though it became a live thing, directly obedient to the iron will which was in command.

They all heard the great walnut log ground and scrape on some jagged stones over which the smaller trunks floated free. Chris saw it roll over, wallowing amongst the others, and breaking up the orderly pattern in which the long rows had been laid. Jacob Woolf thrust it back into its place with his steel-shod pole, so that after the momentary confusion of jostling butts and ends the logs settled back into proper ranks again. There was a fearful minute when the moon was hidden under a cloud and black shadow fell all about them; but the light flooded out once more just as they came into a new stretch of roaring water. At last they shot through the final pool, threaded their way past the furthermost reef and came into the broad, still basin which stretched a mile from shore to shore. The perilous passage for this portion of the raft was over.

They drew into the bank and made lines fast amongst the willows. A poet might have called that reach Peace Pool, but the rivermen had named it Stubbs' Eddy. While the crew completed the task of mooring in the shallow waters next to the bank, Pierre Dumenille thrust the sounding pole overboard.

"How is the water?" asked Woolf, beside him.

"An inch more up and still rising. But even that is none too much."

The voyage had filled some tense hours of exhausting labor; but this was but the beginning. They left two hands in charge, launched the rowboat and set out on the long journey back to the head of the rapids. The skiff was heavily laden; Chris and Stuart sat on one thwart and pulled an oar together. They were taking the boat up a narrow backwater, where the current was slack. But even here it was a long pull, past the island and in and out of the turns of the devious waterway. Presently Pierre Dumenille, sitting in the stern to steer, motioned Chris to take his place.

"I will tell you how to go," he said as he put the tiller ropes into the boy's hand and took his place at the oar. Chris was the youngest in that brawny company; he felt an uncomfortable blush of shame that he was the first to be relieved. But he had to admit within himself that for the moment he could do no more and that Pierre's sharp eye had seen correctly even in the uncertain moonlight. Presently Stuart was assigned to the tiller and Chris returned to his oar, pulling steadily beside Pierre Dumenille up the long miles down which they had slid with all too great a momentum. Almost without looking back over his shoulder, the pilot gave directions as to how the boat was to be steered. It was true, as men said of him, that he could run every reach of the river blindfold. At a certain point, they moored the boat and tramped the last few miles back to where the remainder of the raft had been left.

The moon had dropped down the sky and the red of morning was showing above the distant bluffs. Chris could see the light blue smoke of the Indian camp fires rising along the eastern bank. On the west side, where the row of rafts lay moored, there was a bustle of activity and the red light of cooking fires making ready for breakfast. The water had been rising all night and the passage now would be no more difficult than it always was known to be. It was not luck, but Pierre Dumenille's unerring pilot's instinct which had carried them downstream at the beginning of a rise.

A sheepish, downcast pair of men stood on the bank just above the spot where Con O'Blennes' cook fire was wafting forth the appetizing odors of coffee and bacon. One fellow came shambling down the bank to speak to Dumenille as the pilot once more stepped on board his raft.

"We'd like to go with you now, sir. What happened last night didn't mean anything. You know mighty well we don't want to ship over the rapids with any other pilot."

"You'll not ship, you'll walk," replied Dumenille sharply. "If you want to meet me at the foot of the pool and make the rest of the trip without further trouble, I'll take you on. But we that carried one strip of the raft over will carry the other, and no need to ask aid from you. But you can pick up the boat as you go."

He turned his back upon them and said no more.

After a brief whispered consultation, the two on the bank turned about and trudged disconsolately away southward. It was plain that they knew from experience how little use there was in arguing with Pierre Dumenille. Yet a friend of one of them, as they disappeared behind a clump of willows, called something across the water from one of the other rafts, seeming to feel sure that in the gray light of the morning not even the sharp-eyed pilot could see who had spoken. There was enmity and reluctant admiration in his tone:

"You had as good luck, Pierre Dumenille, as that friend of yours, Joe Langford, that went over twenty-four hours ahead of you."

Pierre Dumenille's face retained its hard calm. He made no reply but directed Con O'Blennes: "Get along with the breakfast. I want the hands to eat before we swing out."

Con's bacon and beans were never more welcome than when served out at the end of that toilsome night. Chris noticed that their commander was still so busy over various matters that the cook had to follow him about to offer him his portion.

"Cast loose," the order came sharply the moment they had finished eating. The crews of the other rafts were also waiting to set out, but the honors of the day

The King of Spain's Daughter

were Pierre Dumenille's and no one would offer to go before him.

It is always easier to do a difficult thing for the second time. Chris found that even though weariness hung heavy upon him, it was far simpler to execute the pilot's commands than on the first passage. Stuart, stationed near him, laughed aloud as they plunged through the first pool and picked their way past the menacing edge of the next reef.

"I'd rather slide down than pull up," he declared. "With daylight to help and a little more water, I'd be glad to run rapids for all the rest of the way."

They passed down this time without even the scrape of a log upon the stones, and floated into Stubbs' Eddy to lie alongside the other portion of the raft. It was a long task to join the two into one again, slow tedious labor punctuated by constant orders and the monotonous squeak of the turning windlasses. After a night without sleep, the nerves and temper of almost every one on board began to wear thin. Stuart, pale with weariness, toiled without a word. Chris was of the sort not easily ruffled, and was able to go steadily about his work. He looked up and laughed when Jacob Woolf swore profusely over the niceties of bringing boom logs exactly into line and of driving home the wooden pegs of the hold-downs.

Swift Rivers

Pierre Dumenille, giving directions from the stern or lending a hand at the point where it was needed, also seemed quite unmoved by the small annoyances of the long task. Soon after, he ordered Chris and Stuart and the others who had worked all night to go into the shelter for some sleep. The boys were both so worn out that their eyes closed instantly. Chris roused once, for a moment, to see, through the tiny window, that the raft, breasting long ripples, was steadily upon its way downstream.

It must have been several hours after that he awoke fully and was surprised to find that they were not moving. Instead they had drawn inshore again and lay beside a bare, red clay bank. Several hundred yards away stood a huddle of cabins about a landing place, where a single brail of logs was moored. And what, what was this — their pilot's figure stepping from the stringpiece to the shore? And why did he carry his coat upon his arm, and a bundle? Chris jumped from his place, hardly even awake, leaped ashore and ran after the striding figure already disappearing over the high clay ridge.

"Pierre, Pierre Dumenille!" He had never called his commander by name before.

Did the tall Frenchman stride on the quicker for a moment, as though he did not mean to hear that summons? An instant after, however, he turned about and stood still in the hot noonday, waiting, but saying no word.

"You're not — you're not going away?"

"But yes," returned Pierre quietly. "Did you not understand? I was not to take you the whole of the voyage."

He made no reference to that other who was now to have the raft in charge, and who was, probably, waiting in the little settlement just below. But the look of utter desolation on the face of Chris Dahlberg, the youth who had come so far and on such a blind, difficult undertaking, seemed suddenly to touch his heart. His black eyes softened as he looked down upon his young friend.

"Do not be so troubled, boy; I am to see you again. Shreve McCloud is in haste to get his logs down the river and so is sending a raft with a younger pilot as far as the head of the rapids. There I am to take it and bring it over, and will follow you all the way downstream. I will be in St. Louis very soon after you. Would you like to seek me out and have some help from me in marketing your wares? We have not done so badly, you and I, in getting the logs, your logs, thus far. I salute you, sir, as one who has conducted himself well in a great venture."

Swift Rivers

He was off, up the bank and out of sight. He would tramp the rude trail back to the last landing place and there would get canoe or rowboat to carry him upstream to meet his raft. Chris, feeling strangely forlorn and bereft, was left standing in the blazing sunshine to look after him as long as his tall figure was still in sight.

There was an hour of waiting in the silent, blinding heat before the new pilot came on board. Joe Langford was as tall a man as Pierre Dumenille; but with that all resemblance ended. He was loose limbed and apparently slow in his movements, although he seemed always to reach his objective with surprising promptness. His orders were given easily and without the Frenchman's sharp decision; he laughed and joked with the men about him in a manner very unlike Dumenille's Indian reticence. Yet to no eyes could it be anything but plain that he was a superlatively good pilot; that he, like his aforetime friend, handled the unwieldy raft with the touch of a master.

Equally plain was it that the man had recently been ill. His face was gaunt and his whole great body pitifully thin. But he made no mention of any such matter and took command with easy confidence.

The raft continued its journey as smoothly and surely as it had before. The passage of the rapids at the mouth of the Des Moines was accomplished without trouble, for there was now a good stage of water. The men of the crew began to talk amongst themselves of the next difficult place, Lone Tree Crossing. That raft which Langford had brought down the river was a small one and had been mostly dispersed among a few little sawmills, set up here and there in the riverside settlements. Only one brail was left and this was joined to the raft turned over by Pierre Dumenille. It made a tremendous structure, but, as all the crew said:

"Joe Langford will handle it if any man can."

They began to meet more boats than in the upper river, for many of the larger vessels did not try to go above the rapids. Some, with no great distance to go, followed the unbelievably difficult method of cordelling, of being towed by a tremendous line, sometimes a thousand feet long, carried by fifteen or twenty men along the bank of the river. There were no tow paths bordering the Mississippi, only brushy shores and wooded points and sloughs, which are branch waterways penetrating the dense woods. Across them the line of struggling men must make their way as best they could.

Other vessels made progress by poling and were built with a covered cargo box in the middle and a plank runway on each side. A man would plant his pole overside at the bow of the boat, set his shoulder against it and walk to the stern, pushing himself almost horizontal in his struggle to thrust the boat forward. Even in the night the travelers on the raft could always know when one of these keel boats was passing, for the tramp, tramp of the heavy boots on the runways would sound afar across the water. All these keel boats were of something the same size and build as a more modern canal boat, though with trimmer lines and finer modeling.

Once and again there would be the unfamiliar sight of a steamboat, a small, clumsy vessel, shaped like the keel boats, puffing upward with great noise and long streams of wood smoke trailing behind it, a marvel indeed amid that laboriously carried commerce.

"When we work our way back, it will probably have to be on a keel boat," Chris would say occasionally. Stuart would make a wry face; for such grinding labor was not of the sort for which he had any taste. He never shirked any task upon the raft, however, and was quicker to understand and obey orders than any other of the crew. Both Pierre Dumenille and Joe Langford openly regarded him as a prized assistant. Langford seemed to enjoy talking to both

The King of Spain's Daughter

boys and giving them new knowledge of the ever-changing river.

"You must know her, waking and sleeping," he said. They both could guess what a long training of hazardous experience had gone to make up the sum of all he knew.

One afternoon, as they were traveling steadily with a brisk breeze behind them, Stuart pointed out to Chris a drift of smoke rising from amongst the trees of a long island. They were used to seeing these gray wisps, scattered thirty and fifty miles apart, but suggesting the pleasant idea of homes and hearthstones and people collected about them.

"But that's a bigger puff than any we have seen," Chris declared. "It looks as though there was something more on fire than just a few sticks at the foot of a mud chimney."

The sharp eyes of Joe Langford were also upon the roll of smoke which went twisting away down the river. "If you like," he said to the two boys, "you can take the boat and go over there to see if there is something wrong. I know the man on that island, Barton Howland. Do anything you can to help him. I believe you can row fast enough to catch us up again."

He stood watching, with his ready, friendly smile,

157

as they let the boat into the water. Chris looked up at him anxiously once before they rowed away. It seemed as though that illness whose mark was left so plainly upon him was not entirely a thing of the past. His eyes looked strangely bright, as though with renewed fever, and his big knees seemed a little unsteady as he walked across the logs. He had heard cheery Con O'Blennes, who had some privileges, say to his superior:

"Say, Captain, ain't you sick?"

He had been silenced so peremptorily that it was not the part of any lesser person to make further comment.

Another thought was also revolving slowly in the boy's mind. Barton Howland — where had he heard the name before — Barton Howland? Yes, that was it, Grandfather had spoken of such a man, who lived in a great house on the bank of the river, with a beautiful wife, and an army of servants. Chris looked doubtfully at the island which they were approaching. It seemed scarcely the place for a mansion. He saw the raft disappearing around a bend. It was the first time that he had let his logs travel without him, since they had set forth, he and they, down the Goose Wing River.

Chris and Stuart pulled across to the island, finding

a stretch of sand at the lower end upon which to draw up the boat. As they turned into a worn path amongst the weeds and willows, a huge, violently grunting pig came charging down upon them, at the top-heavy gallop peculiar to pigs in great agitation. It was followed by others of varying sizes, all running and squealing and crashing through the underbrush in haphazard escape from some danger behind them. The smell of burning grew sharp, and the crackle of flames was now plainly audible, as the boys broke into a run through the willows.

They came into a little clearing in the midst of which was built a log hut with a row of sheds behind it. Flames were licking from the narrow windows and from the door; while just before it a bareheaded man stood staring helplessly at the scene of disaster. He was wavering as though almost overcome by the clouds of hot smoke which swirled about him. But even as the boys came near, he stepped forward blindly as though in desperate determination to enter the burning house.

The two rushed up beside him and caught him, one by each arm. "You cannot go in there," Chris told him sternly, "you can scarcely stand now."

But the owner of the house pressed forward none the less and the boys could do no other than follow him.

He stumbled weakly over the threshold and, quite unable to speak, indicated a big wooden chest which he had dragged halfway across the floor, but had been forced to abandon in the suffocating heat of the room. Stuart and Chris made a plunge within, caught the two rope handles and brought the heavy box out between them, gasping as they came into the fresh air, but bearing it safely to the grass outside. The delight and relief on the man's face were quite recompense enough, for he was still incapable of speaking.

The two boys forced him to sit down upon the grass while they sought for means to put out the fire. There was a well beside the house, with a rude windlass for drawing up the water, and two overturned buckets lying beside it. Chris scrambled to the low eaves of the burning building and from there clambered to the ridge-pole, while Stuart mounted upon a corner of the shed to hand him buckets of water from below. There was already a gaping hole in the roof through which Chris emptied the pails as fast as they came up to him.

The smoke and flame had already lessened a little when the master of the house recovered sufficiently to bear a hand also. The fire was creeping toward the sheds, but he and Stuart threw water across the roof of bark shingles. A corner of the pigsty had caught fire; but Barton Howland had already opened the bars

to let its squealing inhabitants go free. Through an ir-
regular hole between the logs of the farther shed, the
face of a calf looked out. Stuart flung open the door
to let the animal and its snorting mother run to safety
as the pigs had done.

It was a small but fierce conflagration and was not
quenched without great labor on the part of the three.
A great charred hole showed in the roof of the cottage; and inside, when the boys stepped through the
low door, was a forlorn confusion, blackened with
smoke and spread over with ashes and trickling
streams of water. The owner of the house came in and
stood surveying the wreckage with a dismayed countenance.

"I built it with my own hands in the beginning," he
said, "but that was fifteen years ago."

He "lived alone", he presently told them, something
they might easily guess for themselves. More information than that, he did not offer. It was, of course,
a burning question with Chris and Stuart as to what
could have been the heavy treasure contained in the
chest which they had brought out with such difficulty.
They watched impatiently as the owner finally went
over to it and lifted the lid. Stuart gave an astounded
exclamation.

"Only books?" he cried.

"Only books," echoed Howland mildly. He had an odd, quiet face, a shock of white hair and a gentleness of manner most unexpected amid those rough surroundings. "If you lived all by yourself upon this island," he continued, "and had no companion through the lonely days and the long evenings, you would not talk of 'only books.' It is books which hold a man steady in such solitude as this."

Stuart, somewhat abashed, said no more, but helped Chris to carry the precious library in again and set the chest in the corner of the cabin least damaged by the fire. The boys made some shift to help the master of the house restore a semblance of order in the wrecked dwelling.

"It's no use," Stuart finally said to Chris when they happened to be outside together. "Nothing will do any good but to tear the whole roof away and put on some sort of a new one. And we'll have to help him do it," he insisted suddenly. "What he could build fifteen years ago he can't build now. Any one can see that. He's old, Chris, old and helpless."

Chris stood silent, struggling with a rebellious heart. His logs going down the river and he here, kept by this chance misfortune to a total stranger! The man had no right to be helpless. Grandfather wouldn't be, and he was far older. Grandfather . . . A thought pushed itself in upon his unworthy hesitation. What would Alexis Dahlberg think was the right thing to do? Chris turned about and walked back toward the house.

"Yes," he said to Stuart. "Of course we have to help him. Joe Langford intended that we should. We will get back to the raft any way we can."

Mr. Howland received the news of their decision with a gratitude which was almost pitiful. "I was wondering," he confessed, "whatever would happen if the rain came in on my books and papers before I had managed to rebuild the roof." Of shelter for his own white head he seemed to have no thought.

The task was a longer one than either of the boys had thought. All the next day they labored, and to the late afternoon of the next. Barton Howland was eager to do his share, but proved to be of no very great use for such an undertaking as this.

As they worked together he explained just what was the cause of the fire. "When I want to send letters or order supplies, I make a smoke signal to the first raft or keel boat that passes," he told them. "I saw your raft miles away, rounding the bend, and I lit the little brush heap I always keep ready. It seemed to be burning very nicely so I went inside to write a letter or two. In the absorption of composition, I must confess that I forgot the fire. Suddenly I found that it had crept through the grass, taken a shed and had attacked the roof. It was fortunate, very fortunate indeed, that Joe Langford sent you to me."

There was also much interesting talk of other matters while the work went forward. Mr. Howland knew how to put shrewd, provocative questions. In half a day's acquaintance he seemed to have come to understand completely that restless Stuart Hale and his wish to "find things, or build something nobody ever thought of building before," and that impatience of his, not of study, but of the authority over their students of professors whom he deemed no wiser than himself.

"I don't like people to tell me what I must do," he declared.

Of Chris, their new friend asked fewer questions, but after hearing about Grandfather, whom he remembered well, and of the logs and the great project, he seemed to be pondering long and deeply.

At last the roof of willow poles and bark shingles was completed, a more weatherproof affair than the one he had put up himself, Mr. Howland admitted. It was got in place just in time to shelter them from a brisk thunder shower. They were sitting at supper after the last work was done, an astonishing supper to the boys who, after Con O'Blennes' salt beef and beans, felt that it was a feast for kings to have set before them fresh fruits and vegetables, home cured bacon and fine white bread. Mr. Barton Howland was a surprisingly excellent cook.

"I have studied the delicacies of all countries," he observed modestly. "Thus I should know something of how to reproduce them."

He fell now to asking steady, purposeful questions of Chris about that region where the boy lived, of which he himself had heard first from Alexis Dahlberg. He nodded several times in smiling satisfaction over what he learned.

"That valley must lie near to the very limits of the Louisiana Purchase." He flung up his head and went on with the fire of enthusiasm in his eyes. "The whole empire of Jefferson's purchase was bought from France, but it belonged, through the most of its history, to the crown of Spain. Beautiful it is beyond words, with its rivers, its woods, its treasures of mines and of furs, its plains where grain can grow, enough to feed the whole world. I like, in my heart, to call that province the King of Spain's daughter, for the King of Spain never had a fairer realm. The name is out of an old song, such a thing as comes back to you in the solitude of the wilderness and sings itself over and over." He fell into further reflection and seemed to be unconscious that he was humming the tune aloud. Chris could not forbear humming with him:

"The King of Spain's daughter, she came to visit me,
And all for the sake of my little nut tree."

The boy wondered if he could tell this stranger how the same air had sung itself through his childhood and had given a name to the walnut tree by the cabin door. He did not try to put his small tale into words. But the look of comprehension in his eager, blue eyes caught Howland's notice and was answered with a smile of understanding.

"I think it very important," the man said, "that some one in high places should know of the wealth and abundance of that valley which lies so far to the north that it is at the very border of the Purchase. We of the United States have been very vague and careless. For a long time we did not know just what was the southern limit to what we had bought, and it is not yet decided where the upper boundary between our territory and Canada is to lie."

He seemed to be pursuing some important thought within his own mind, for it was a space of minutes before he went on:

"We have a just claim to every tributary to the Mississippi, but it may easily happen that wise statesmen, knowing nothing of the matter, will think that a few hundred miles of wild forest land here or there are of little importance and will allow this rich possession, timber and ore and farming land, to pass into other hands. I will write," he concluded reflectively, "let me see, to whom had I better write, to draw attention to such a matter? I believe it were better to turn directly to the President. Andrew Jackson is an old friend of mine, though I have not brought myself much to his notice in his latter, busy years. But I will write to him at once, so that you can take the letter and send it by the mail which goes eastward from Saint Louis."

He seemed to think that it was no matter for explanation that a man in that lonely cabin should sit down to write familiarly to a President. He brought paper from the cupboard and began, his quill pen scratching steadily over one sheet after another. He looked up now and again to ask clever, specific questions: how many farms in the Goose Wing Valley were cleared, was there more pine than other wood, was the walnut plentiful — walnut begins to be in great demand — were there other minerals besides iron?

"I think not much but iron," Stuart told him, "although I had hopes, myself, that there might be gold."

"I am not sure but that the world needs iron somewhat more than gold," Howland returned smiling, as his pen moved on again. There was a brightness upon his face which only real knowledge and intelligence can bring to any countenance. Chris watched it wistfully; it stood for his greatest desire beyond the immediate need of caring for Grandfather. The man looked up suddenly and seemed to read that longing on the boy's open face.

"How much have you been to school?" he demanded suddenly.

"Only a little," Chris answered him. He did not feel shy in the presence of this sincerely interested acquaintance. "There was a neighborhood school in our valley in the winter time. For a year or two a man took charge of it who lived in our region because he loved it, and not because he could not earn a far better living elsewhere. He gave me extra teaching in the evenings; Uncle Nels was willing when he found it cost nothing. So I am lucky enough to have learned a little more than there was the usual chance to do. But some day when Grandfather has a comfortable, warm house and peace and safety for the rest of his life, then — then I am going to learn something more."

Stuart Hale got up and went to stand in the door

looking out at the soft green willows growing all about the cabin and at a blue stretch of river visible beyond. Had it cost him a pang of shame to hear his comrade talk with such longing of the chance for education which he had so easily thrown away? Neither of the other two took note of him, however; for the master of the cabin and Chris were in absorbed talk.

"I will give you a letter to a man I know in St. Louis; he can tell you just what a lad of your desire and promise must do to find more learning. He will put his whole heart into the matter, or I do not know David Payne."

It was while the second letter was being written that Chris had a sudden thought. "Why," he exclaimed to Stuart, "we cannot catch up with Langford, but we do not need to row all the way down the river. Pierre Dumenille will be passing down with the second raft; we can go on with him." A sudden panic seized him lest their friend should have gone by in the night. But no, he would not have time to come, all that distance, until the next day at the earliest.

"Pierre Dumenille," repeated Mr. Howland, looking up from his letter. "Ah, I am glad you know him, as well as Joe Langford. I wish — " he sighed. "I wish just what all of us wish who like and admire them both."

Chris was watching almost before dawn next day for the appearance of Pierre Dumenille. It was well into the morning, however, before the long line of the raft came into view around the bend and the boys could put off in their boat to join it. Their new friend gave them a great basket of young peas and fresh eggs, a side of bacon and a quantity of early red raspberries. The letters Chris bestowed carefully in an inner pocket, looking first in renewed wonder at the superscription upon one of them, "The President of the United States."

Pierre Dumenille opened his eyes in astonishment at seeing his former assistants appear out of nowhere, and laden with such strange gifts. The men of the raft were full of enthusiasm for such an addition to their fare, and, over the midday meal, told the boys something of the man to whom they had given such timely aid.

"A queer duck," they described Barton Howland, "a fellow that nobody knows what to make of. He came into this new country with some of the first settlers and built what was a big, grand house for these parts, not so far above the Rock Island Rapids. But something happened, I never rightly heard just what, and he went away to live by himself on what's come to be called Howland's Island. They say he makes out pretty well, that he raises everything he needs, and keeps his house as neat as a woman would. You'd never think that he came of people who had an army of black servants and didn't think it was right to do a hand's turn of work themselves."

Later in the evening Pierre Dumenille told them a little more of this strange dweller on the willow-bordered island. "There was a sickness that went all over this North country," he said, "and it stole into big houses just the same as into the cabins. His young wife and his two little sons died within a week, and he rode away from the place and never would go back to it again. But it's not right," Pierre added, vigorously stuffing tobacco into his black, violently smelling pipe, "it's not right for a man who could do great things to go away and live so, all by himself, no matter what was the sorrow that he has seen."

Pierre made no reference to the pilot with whom the boys had been sailing. All he said was:

"When the right time comes, you had better take the boat back to the raft to which it belongs. And Chris will wish to travel with his logs."

There was one more day and night of uneventful floating, with the smooth river sliding below them, with the brilliant, summer stars swinging overhead in the warm darkness. Just before dusk, Pierre and

Stuart had been ashore to get supplies at a farm near the shore. When they returned, Stuart had something odd to tell his comrade.

"The farmer had some report that we couldn't understand, brought by an Indian who came in to sell him berries. Something about trouble down at Lone Tree Crossing, but such vague talk we could not make anything of it."

The night was without a breeze and very hot, so that few could sleep and all longed for the rain which might bring a breath of freshness to the heavy air. Chris, lying in his place, could see Pierre Dumenille prowling restlessly about the raft, as though heat, or troubled thoughts, made slumber impossible. Toward morning the shower came, a steady, windless downpour which wrapped the moving craft in a gray curtain. Suddenly, from out of the dim, wet twilight, a voice sounded and a boat came into view, a trader's canoe with a single man in it. What he was calling to them was half lost in the sound of the rain beating steadily upon the logs:

"Have you heard what happened at Lone Tree Crossing? Joe Langford — smashed his raft — split all in pieces on the bar — "

Pierre Dumenille spun about in his place at the stern.

The King of Spain's Daughter

"What is that?" he cried, stung out of his Indian reticence at last. "Say that again, man." The others gathered hastily to listen for a reply.

The trader had evidently not known that it was Pierre Dumenille to whom he had brought tidings. As though in dismay at the sudden knowledge of what this news must mean, he sheered away. He called something over his shoulder which no one could catch, and vanished into the rain. Pierre, with a face set and quiet again, gave an order which sent every man to his place.

He must have seen how heads were laid together and how talk flew from one to another, but he made no sign. They floated serenely on, past green islands and wooded bays, with no possibility of hastening even if the commander in the stern had wished it. After that first moment of outburst, no word or look gave indication that he had any knowledge of what had occurred.

"We're all speculating," one of the men said to the boys after supper, drawing at his pipe and speaking low, lest the sharp ears of Dumenille might hear, "we're speculating whether Pierre will go past Joe Langford in trouble or whether he'll stop to help him. There never were friends like those two were friends, in the time before the falling out. If you've hurt a

Frenchman, he may forgive you, especially if he finds you in distress. But if you hurt an Indian, he hates you forever. And we none of us know which Pierre Dumenille will prove himself to be."

During the next day, while Chris and Stuart were at their places at the sweeps, they held snatches of conversation together between the moments when it was necessary to swing the head of the raft.

"I believe he will go by," Stuart declared. "Perhaps Dumenille has been waiting all this time for just the minute when he can show Langford what he truly thinks of him."

Chris pondered and was not so sure. He recollected that first meeting, so long ago now, when those words had dropped from Pierre without his own volition: "I hoped to forget that I had quarreled with my dearest friend."

"I couldn't guess what he will do," he said to Stuart. "And if you were in his place, how would it be with you?"

"Oh, I would go sailing by, and not even look about to watch how Langford took it," Stuart replied instantly. Then after a moment's pause he was obliged to add, "I'm not so absolutely sure, Chris, that I would after all. Perhaps no person really knows enough about himself to say which way he will turn until the time comes. There was your Uncle Nels who treated you rather worse than Joe Langford treated Pierre. And yet Eric Knudson told me — "

Chris turned suddenly to dip his sweep with an awkward splash, such as so practised an oarsman as he had become should never have perpetrated. He carried the discussion no further. Of one thing he could not speak, nor could Stuart. If the raft was smashed, were the logs lost — the logs of Chris and Alexis Dahlberg?

Through the whole of the day, every eye was strained forward, every sense on the alert. Never had their mode of travel seemed more unbearably slow. The river was growing ever wider and the banks more level. Long ago they had passed the last white trunks of birches; instead they saw now great banks of close foliage which stood for elm, scrub oak and hickory. Of these, however, Chris took no note; for his mind was upon one thing only. It was toward evening that they rounded a final bend and saw a line of red flares stretching, so it seemed, far out into the river. It was even as the passing trader had reported. Joe Langford and his raft had gone aground at Lone Tree Crossing.

As they floated closer, they saw that the long bar of sand lay in an elbow of the channel, just where a cross wind and the slightest awkwardness in handling would bring a raft into peril. And into this peril, the fortune of the river had flung Joe Langford headlong and his command with him.

It was not until they came very near that they could see, in the fading light, the true magnitude of the disaster. The raft lay across the bar like a crumpled piece of paper, just where the wind and the water had thrown it. Only a scant third of it still floated; the rest was smashed and split upon the shelving sands, the booms torn asunder and the logs set free and flung in fantastic piles all up and down the shore. A few loose timbers were afloat; and even as Chris was watching, he saw a group of black trunks slide into the water and go bobbing away. His logs, the fruit of his toil! He looked everywhere but could catch no glimpse of the big walnut tree. His mind felt stunned and numb: he could think dully of but a single question, unimportant in the midst of the great disaster:

"Has the little nut tree been rescued?"

"The low water has saved most of the timber so far," a raftsman said as he stood watching beside the boys. "But with every inch the river comes up, there will be more to get away. I'm certainly sorry for Joe Langford."

They came nearer; they were abreast of the wreck. Almost involuntarily every man took his place beside his steering sweep, awaiting the command to swing in. The crew on the broken raft were shouting to them; one lifted a torch from its socket and waved it about his head. But Pierre Dumenille stood unmoving in the stern and his craft floated on. They were passing. They were fairly by.

"He won't leave them — he can't," Chris cried fiercely to himself. Just at that instant the quick order came:

"Head her in."

The raft turned about in a long curve, came to a standstill in an eddy, and lay along the shore.

"Make fast," Dumenille directed, "and put the boat over the side. Chris, you and Stuart are to take the oars."

As they pulled across to the bar, the last of the light died behind them, so that it was quite dark when the boys laid the skiff alongside the stranded raft. The man with the torch came to meet them and stood holding it above his head to shine down into the boat. It was Jacob Woolf.

"We would never have broke up like this, if Joe Langford had been handling her," he said. "But he's not known any one since the evening after we passed Howland's Island."

"Why don't you pick up your logs, man?" demanded Pierre impatiently. "You'll lose them all if you don't set to it."

"Seems sort of heartless, to be out chasing logs and him — " Jacob jerked his head toward the shelter in the stern, "and him — going."

"Going?" It was Dumenille who echoed the word. Chris, sitting so close to the stern seat that his knee touched that of Pierre, felt a quiver run through that big frame.

"Yes, going," Woolf repeated. He spoke stolidly, but his voice was belied by a sudden working of his hard, leathery face. "He lies there and asks just for two things, first water and then Pierre Dumenille."

The boat gave such a sudden jerk that both the boys caught the boom logs to keep it from capsizing. It was only because their commander had leaped so suddenly from his place. The two sat looking at the loose logs, which dipped a little still from the pressure of those rapidly running feet. They saw Pierre lift the canvas curtain that closed the door of the pilot's shelter.

"Joe!" they heard him cry out in a voice such as no man had ever known him to use before. "Joe, my friend, my friend!"

CHAPTER VI

LONE TREE CROSSING

Joe Langford, a wasted giant, lay on the board flooring at the stern of his broken raft, with the sweet night air blowing clean above him. With rough well-meaning, his men had done their best for him. Their efforts had not been entirely wise. Several of them knew vaguely of its being a well-established idea that a patient with fever must not have water to drink. They were also convinced of the danger of draughts, and had covered him up in the rude raft shanty, and hung a heavy tarpaulin before the door. They could not keep out all of the fresh river air which blew in through the curtain, nor were their hearts hard enough to deny, too often, the sick man's constant plea for water. With all they could do, the fever waxed and life waned, until it seemed indeed, that night, that Joe Langford was going.

There was probably no more keenly observing eye on the river than Pierre Dumenille's, not only for currents and landmarks, but for men. He took the

179

accurate measure of every person who came near him; knew just what that person could do and where he would be of the greatest use. For fifteen minutes after he first lifted the heavy curtain, Pierre remained silent within that stifling space in the presence of his friend. Then he spoke through the door to the nearest man waiting outside:

"Send Stuart Hale here."

From where Chris waited in the boat, holding himself ready to bring any further help which the others thought that he might give, he could hear faintly the voices of the two who were working over Joe Langford. He overheard Stuart's voice saying:

"I would sponge him with cold water. Whatever people say, it stands to reason that a man who is burning up needs to be cooled. And we must exchange these clothes for something else."

There was a long pause broken by few words and only by the sound of feet moving back and forth and the cool splash of water. Finally Chris was told to pull back to Dumenille's raft, to bring some garments crudely clean after a washing in the river, and to fetch some other supplies from the pilot's chest. Later, after he had returned, he helped to carry the sick man out into the free air, and laid him where a sheet of white canvas had been spread upon the boards. Then he, and even Stuart, took themselves away to wait beside the boat and leave that long night watch to be spent by those two friends alone.

Jacob Woolf sat beside the boys and offered bits of information and comment in a whisper, from time to time, as the hours drew by:

"Langford was wise enough to ship a helper at that first town after Howland's Island. The fellow, Ned Kelly, knew the river tolerably well; what he didn't know was how to handle a raft. Lone Tree Crossing is the shallowest spot a craft has to navigate on the whole trip; you've heard that — every one has. It is worse than the rapids, except that you're over it in a minute, unless you don't get over at all."

He left them, to go upon a round of inspection, which he pursued at regular intervals, but which accomplished little save to reveal that more and more logs were escaping through the smashed booms. Con O'Blennes came presently to sit down heavily near by and to give, in snatches, further account of what had happened:

"It takes one head, and a whole lot of hands to hold a raft steady when the wind catches it. That was all it was, a gust of wind coming before a thunder shower, and we in just the place where it could wreck us. The young fellow did his best, but he couldn't handle the men or the raft. Just a minute we hung shivering, and then the crashing and the smashing began and the current was breaking all our booms to pieces. I don't think Joe Langford even knew it had happened."

The night went by, lit by stars, and presently by a late cloudy moon. Con O'Blennes fell into silence finally, so that the stillness was broken only by small sounds, the logs scraping together and the slight splash as one after another lifted free and floated away. There were subdued voices in the distance as the raft hands occasionally consulted one with another. The muttering and occasional crying out of the sick man was hushed; for it seemed that he had fallen into something like slumber. Stuart and Chris finally lay down also and dozed a little, but never fell really asleep as they waited the night out.

Chris lay looking the length of the long, flat sand bank, and saw it reveal itself slowly as the darkness began to fade, showing the dark heaps of logs and the white sand. At the end of the bar rose the outstretched arms of the great blasted tree which had given the difficult place its name. The red flares which were kept burning to warn any other craft away from the broken wreck, were allowed to go down, since, now that day was coming, all men could see what had happened to Joe Langford and his raft. It was just as the last red flame winked and went out that Chris sat up suddenly to listen. He heard a voice which had not sounded before, other than with the unrecognizable incoherence of delirium. But now Joe Langford, as though awakened from real sleep, was speaking clearly:

"Pierre Dumenille, is it you?"

There was joy enough in those brief words, so it seemed, to carry a man back on a returning tide of life even though it had dropped to its very lowest ebb.

It was at noon that day when Pierre Dumenille, Stuart and Chris held consultation in the pilot's shelter of Dumenille's raft. There always arrives a moment in the history of friendship, when the reserves and questions and the sounding of one another's natures come to an end, and complete understanding takes their place. Pierre talked to the two boys with a frankness which took for granted that all three of them had the same desire and would bend themselves to the same effort.

"I have got to go on," he told them. "Chris, even in spite of the disaster to your logs, I must go on. You know that. I take it for granted that you understand."

The boy nodded. He realized fully that if Langford were to have any chance of recovery, he must be carried forward at once.

"I think," said Pierre slowly, "I am certain that the good God is going to let my friend live. But we must do our share to save him. Since you comprehend that, we must now settle the question of what to do to rescue the raft." He paused for the space of a breath and looked each of the boys in turn straight in the eyes.

"Stuart, you have a quick eye and a quick mind; you can see in a flash how a thing ought to be done. But you are not always good at carrying out an enterprise. Your temper is as quick as your eye; unless you can hold it, you get nowhere with the men about you. Chris is not so quick; instead he has the faculty of keeping to a thing until it is done. He is shy, he holds back from having to do with those around him, because he has lived a life which did not have many strangers in it. He has a gift, just the same, for handling men; they see his honesty and the straightness of his purpose and they follow him. I am telling you this concerning yourselves, because there will be work in your hands which will take your whole power to accomplish."

There could be no question that he had summed up completely the strength and weakness of each of those

two before him. Chris understood now why Pierre
Dumenille had sent him alone to bring back their
reluctant crew. On winning that victory Chris had
felt something as he had that day when he cut the
meadow alone.

Stuart had not flinched under Pierre's plain speaking. "I know you are right," he agreed. "I have always
taken things up and dropped them again as soon as
they were hard or I lost my temper. I have never
pushed one single thing to its finish. I begin to see that,
unless I do it now, perhaps I never will. I am ready to
put my hand to whatever work you say, and I give
you my promise that I will follow it until it is done."

"It is a heartbreaking task that I am going to give
you," Dumenille returned, "one that all river men
dread as they dread nothing else. It is to gather up
scattered logs driven by the wind and current, to work
long hours under the hot sun and with the help of
clumsy men who cannot move or think as quickly as
you. Ned Kelly, that apprentice pilot that Langford
took with him, knows something of how the thing
should be done, but he is not the man to have enough
force to accomplish it. I will give you both full directions, where you must lay a floating boom from the
shore and how to drive the logs in behind it as you
catch them one by one. The men themselves know

Swift Rivers

something of how to repair the frames and set the brails in order again. The question is this," he was speaking, now, directly to Stuart Hale, "do you undertake this willingly, the thing which is to be done for the sake of this friend of both of us, Chris Dahlberg?"

There could be, indeed, no doubt of what the boy would answer. Stuart, with his dark eyes unwaveringly set upon the pilot's even blacker ones, said steadily:

"You offered me my chance back there at the Goose Wing, and I told myself then I would make good for you."

"But this is a larger and longer work than you thought you were undertaking," Dumenille insisted; but Stuart only replied:

"It is a bigger chance, and I promise myself and you that I will not turn away from it."

"Good, good!" Pierre's thin face beamed with pleasure. And then he added with that absolute simplicity which perhaps only a man of Indian blood could possibly achieve, "I should like to put down on paper for you all the instructions which I shall need to give. But perhaps you may not know — I do not read or write. Men born just as I have been do not have any

186

great chance for learning much besides what the woods and the river can teach them."

He passed over the matter quickly and gave neither of the boys opportunity to speak. Chris could scarcely believe that, in a man of Pierre Dumenille's extraordinary attainments, there should be such a tragic want. But Pierre, warning them that they must remember carefully just what he said, plunged into a detailed description of exactly what must be done to salvage the broken raft, how the logs must be collected and re-enclosed, and how the stranded portion must be pulled off the bar. The only means of getting it free was by fastening lines to some immovable object and winding them up upon the windlasses, until the heavy weight of the raft was pulled off the sand, by main force, into the water.

"Should we hitch the ropes to the Lone Tree?" Stuart asked him, but Dumenille advised against their doing that. The great trunk stood in the wrong place.

"The tree, moreover, is dead, and though it may stand a great many years longer to guide pilots over this difficult way, it might not hold against such a strain. And you would pull it down," he said. "No, the raft hands will show you how to bury a big log deep in the sand on the bank above, with stakes about it so that scarcely any power on earth will pull it up again. The river men call it 'putting down a dead man'."

When, next day, Pierre Dumenille took his friend on board his raft, cast loose from the willows and sailed away, it seemed to the boys left behind that a vast amount of their courage and strength had gone away with him. The magnitude of what they had before them never seemed quite so clear as when they stood on the edge of the Lone Tree Bar and watched their friend's craft slip around the next bend and disappear. On the upper Mississippi one seldom sees any vessel diminished to a dot in the distance; there is always a turn between green bluffs to carry it quickly out of sight.

Ned Kelly, the cub pilot, two or three years older than Stuart, was nominally in charge. He proved to be a man of little ability, but of a great deal of easy good nature. He was glad enough to have any aid which could be offered; nor was there ever any question amongst them of divided authority. The men understood immediately that the quick brain of Stuart Hale and the steady force of Chris Dahlberg would be the real means of accomplishing the saving of the raft, if it were to be accomplished. They had all been devoted to Joe Langford; they had admired his unflinching fight against deadly illness, as he tried to bring his craft to port. They were all willing to do their best for the salvage of the logs for which he was responsible. Their really belonging to Chris did not seem a matter of great moment. Every one knew that there was no longer or more disheartening task than the reassembling of a scattered raft. It was, however, one of the misadventures which come in the way of a river man's life; and all accepted it with the mere comment that this trip was an especially unlucky one.

They began forthwith to link together some of the biggest remaining logs, rowed them downstream and attached one end of the string to the shore at the spot selected by Pierre Dumenille. Into this pocket between shore and boom they began to shoot the floating trunks which were drifting here, there and everywhere. The rise in the water level made some portions of the work easier, but some of it infinitely harder. A number of the logs, with inanimate perversity, had managed to drift into the edge of the woods, a tangled scrub of willow and slippery elm, where it was most difficult to recover them.

Everyone worked long, hour after hour, with Chris or Stuart in command of the boat which pursued the logs, with the raft foreman at the end of the floating boom superintending the final capture of the fugitives, and with Ned Kelly in charge of the boring and coupling of those timbers which were to make up the new brails. The days were hot and breathless; the nights were sultry; the work dragged and seemed as though it would never come to an end.

They had spectators at their work, of which at first they were scarcely conscious. Some miles below Lone Tree Bar, a large creek ran into the Mississippi upon whose bank was an Indian village. At first these red neighbors watched from afar; later they grew bolder and came close, seeming to have not much other occupation than to slip in and out of the underbrush on the bank and observe what the white men were doing. A few paddled round the point of the bar in their canoes; all of them seemed consumed with interest and curiosity.

They appeared to have neither awe nor any great admiration for this company of whites who had got themselves into such grievous trouble, and who seemed so strangely determined to get themselves out of it. Indians, under any circumstances that might be considered similar, would have cheerfully abandoned the wreckage of all their earthly possessions and have gone away and forgotten the disaster. Chris liked to watch them bobbing about in their skilfully managed dugout canoes. The boats were fashioned by shaping and hollowing cedar logs, since here there was no birch bark to be obtained such as the Chippewa used for their lighter and more graceful vessels.

White men came that way also, for after a day or two, a keel boat went by. It was laden with furs, wool and farm produce from the scattered homesteads along the river. The crew paused to offer generous assistance; but there were in actual truth enough hands to do the work. All that was really needed was a vast store of patience and endurance. To this the well-meaning passers-by added nothing, for their frank counsel was to abandon the wreck and let the river take it.

"When a raft is piled up like that one, it's not to be got together again. I never heard of its being done," the pessimistic pilot assured Chris and Stuart. "And that Ned Kelly that's in charge, he's a good steersman, but he don't know nothing beyond that. He'll be no help to you. You'd better get aboard and we'll carry you to St. Louis."

To this well-meant offer the boys returned emphatic refusal. The keel boat men, therefore, departed upon their way. A few traders in canoes went by also, each one stopping to offer sympathetic comment and a great deal of advice.

"If another well-informed river man tells me what

to do, I'm going to kill him," Stuart observed vindictively at last. "Pierre Dumenille gave us enough instructions in the beginning; we haven't asked every fellow that comes this way to stop and tell us what he thinks about it."

Chris could see that Stuart's small store of patience had wasted to an end, had been renewed by his determination to keep his promise, but had worn thin over and over again. Even he himself, who had a greater stake than any of the others in the affair, was growing unbelievably discouraged.

There was one morning with the sun coming up burning and cloudless just as it had risen day after day. The surface of the water was like hot metal. The crew was assembled at daylight to eat a tasteless breakfast. Even Con O'Blennes' clean fare had deteriorated somewhat. Chris Dahlberg's anxious eyes noted that Stuart left his share untasted. Even the others ate listlessly, since the heat, even at that hour, was sufficient to deaden all energy. One of them broke out suddenly, in a tone which he might have been trying to control but which none the less sounded sharp and querulous:

"I've lost count of the days but it does seem to me that it's about time for it to be a Sunday. I'm sick of chasing logs that ain't there, and I'm going to lay off, anyway until night."

This was a matter for Ned Kelly to settle and he did it in the least difficult way. "Why yes, I was kind of thinking, myself, that Sunday was about due. A bit of a rest won't hurt any of us, and logs won't float any faster on one day than another."

It may have been an unwise decision, but at least it averted immediate and serious trouble. What that good-natured consent might be storing up in the way of insubordination on the morrow was not possible to guess.

With the cessation of all labor, the small irritations and the weary exaggeration of grievances seemed to grow suddenly very great. Through the long idle morning, as the men lay about in such patches of shade as could be found, there was the sound of a half dozen petty quarrels, which flared up and died out again.

Chris and Ned Kelly sat on one of the broken booms, which was half buried in the dry sand, to count over what amount of timber the raft had lost. Scarcely a third of the logs afloat had been recovered. A certain number could be accounted for as having stranded in difficult and inaccessible refuges along the shore, and could be got back with sufficient expenditure of time and effort. But a very great quantity, representing much of the value of the raft, had disappeared entirely. The timbers had all been stamped and counted before the raft was made up in the beginning, so that, by looking over the tallies, it was possible to tell just which ones were gone.

"A good many of them are those red logs from the woods above Cedar River," Ned Kelly said. "Langford picked up a brail of them as we were coming down, and said to me that they were about the most valuable of any of the stuff he was taking along. It will be a bad thing for me and my standing with McCloud, if so many of them are lost."

Chris got up, his body, and even, it seemed, his very spirit, trembling in a sudden gust of tremendous feeling. He could scarcely call it anger, it was too great for that. Ned Kelly could prate of the handful of cedar logs which were gone and could worry about his standing with Shreve McCloud, with no mention of the magnitude of the disaster which had come to Chris Dahlberg! Did he not know what labor, what hope were bound up in that venture upon which Chris had set out? Was he blind to what the boy must feel to see his chance of success flung to destruction by the hand of another? For the life of him Chris could think of nothing to say that would meet such an occasion, so that he could only walk, unseeing, along the hot sand, away from the raft, away from Ned Kelly and his small-hearted lamentations, away from everything.

For nearly half a mile he tramped along the sun-beaten bar, and stopped in the tiny patch of shade under the great dead tree at the outer end. He heard the sound of rowlocks and a voice behind him. Stuart, with one of the boats, had come rowing across the stretch of water and had set the skiff's bow against the sand.

"Get in," he said briefly.

Chris slipped into the forward seat and took the oar which the other relinquished to him. He felt that he could not sit in the stern; he wished, at that moment, to look into nobody's face. But as they rowed away together, he felt a little comfort stealing over the soreness of his misery. No matter what happens, it is of help, always, to have a true friend.

They dropped down the river, half a mile, nearly a mile. Only a few times had they gone so far in pursuit of their logs, for there were bends and beaches everywhere upon which the fugitives were almost certain to catch. All those which they had found at all were ashore within a quarter of a mile of the disaster. The rest had vanished without even a scattering of stragglers to mark their progress downstream. But since neither of the boys had any wish to return to their bickering comrades on the sandbar, they went rowing steadily forward. They had gone a long way before Stuart announced suddenly:

"I have made a guess as to where the walnut tree and the others have gone."

Chris did not answer, although he was beginning to have some vague surmise of his own. He was for the moment too weary, too heavy of heart, to fix his mind upon anything. But the thought grew insistent so that, after a little, as though to test his own guess by that of his companion, he said indifferently:

"We are getting rather close to the Indians' creek. Pierre warned us to keep out of the way of the village." He recollected very vividly that one of Dumenille's special instructions had been:

"Do not have any trouble with the Indians. It would be serious for you. Moreover it would be bad for every man that comes after you down the river. Some groups of Indians are friendly; some are indifferent; but some obstinately hostile. This village of red men has a bad reputation even among their own kind. It is well to keep away from them yourselves and by all means to prevent the raftsmen from going near. If they do, there will be an outbreak at once."

Lone Tree Crossing

All this Stuart must surely remember. And must he not remember also that incident in the North woods, where even a friendly Chippewa chief had burst forth in wrath and threatened his life? Nevertheless he kept rowing on, and Chris, with a dawning grin of comprehension, pulled steadily with him.

They brought the boat to shore some hundreds of yards above the inflowing of the tributary creek, which came in on the west side of the Mississippi. It was broad and sluggish, bordered with willows, like every such watercourse, but appearing to be deeper than a good many of the rivulets which dropped into the vastness of the main stream. The two, evidently in one mind without need of speech, pulled the skiff out of sight into a clump of willow brush and slid into the soft green thicket which fringed the bank.

They made their way cautiously among the close-tangled stems, advancing with a care and silence which would have done credit to the red men themselves. A long, hot journey it was, nearly two miles over rough ground, always wrapped in the soft concealing cloud of willow foliage. Stuart was ahead and suddenly stopped, motioning to Chris for complete quiet.

They could look through an opening in the undergrowth and see, almost opposite them, the Indian village. Very still and empty it was at that time of day, with the braves away hunting or fishing and only the women to tend the tumbling children and the fires. The creek, which lay between the boys and the group of pointed lodges, was very broad here, three hundred feet across at the least. And the whole surface of it was covered with logs. In the middle, possibly aground even in that depth, looming enormous amongst the other trunks, was the little nut tree.

Not every warrior, however, had gone to hunt that day. As the boys lay in the underbrush watching, one Indian came striding down the worn trail to the foot of the bank just across from them. He was making sure, evidently, that the precious logs were all safe. He launched a wooden canoe and paddled carefully back and forth among the captive flotilla, pushing one log here and turning back another there, to be certain that none should drift away in the slow current of the creek. He passed very close to where the boys were concealed, so that they could see his face plainly, a harsh, cruel countenance, very different from that of the Indians with whom Chris was familiar.

He was used to the quiet and outwardly friendly Chippewa who had lived at peace with two generations of white settlers. He had not thought that it would be a matter of great difficulty to recover the stolen property from the pilfering red men; it would not have been so with the northern people. But here was an affair of much greater import, as he realized with the sudden miss of a heartbeat. They had to do now with sullen savages who needed but little excuse to break out into flaming hostility.

The canoe went on, threading its way through the mass of trunks which bumped and chafed together as they all lay lazily afloat in the willow-fenced pool. Chris saw the man pass close to the great walnut tree and lay his hand upon it to feel the rough texture of its bark. Some of the logs the Indians could make into canoes, though they never could find use for all of them. There was nothing that they could do with Grandfather's beloved tree, since they must soon discover that, without the spruce stems pinned to it, the great mass would not float, and that their rude tools could do little with its tough wood. They would burn it, perhaps, in some ceremonial fire, and exult, as they did so, in the feat of outwitting the white men. Was it for this that Grandfather had so courageously cut it down — Grandfather who had said that Chris Dahlberg's road to fortune was to set out from the foot of the little nut tree?

Stuart whispered softly into his friend's ear. "We can't do anything until the dark comes."

Chris nodded agreement. When the Indian had

landed and disappeared over the ridge of the opposite bank, the boys slipped noiselessly away and came back to their boat. They embarked in silence and pulled upstream.

"I don't care to go back to that idle, snarling lot on the raft," Stuart said finally. "I brought some food, and we will just land somewhere and wait until night. Shall we climb the bluff across from the bar? I have wanted to have time to go up there ever since we began our work at Lone Tree Crossing."

They pulled past the tip of the bar, crossed the stretch of rapid current and came into the shade of the hill. It was graciously cool after the hot blaze of the sun on the water. They brought the boat to a landing and noticed a faint trail leading up through the bushes toward the top of the bluff, made by deer, perhaps, who grazed above and came down at nightfall to drink. The two had, so far, had no time to explore anything but the low reaches of shore where the logs lay. Without more ado they jumped out of the boat, made it fast, and set out to climb the almost indiscernible path.

They were scarcely prepared for what they saw when they reached the summit. It was so high that they could look, to the eastward, over the windings of the Mississippi, over the low lands opposite and across to the glint of crooked streams, where tributaries wandered through the green and emptied into the river. But it was not that view of islands and waters at which both boys stood gazing, for their eyes were turned to the west. Chris had heard men speak of the prairie, lying beyond the hills which bordered the river. It was just here that the prairie reached forward and came to the very edge of the Mississippi bluffs.

Even at home in his own wooded valley he had heard talk of the vast plains country which was so utterly different from the northern region of hill and forest. Here he could look upon it at last, a tremendous stretch of rolling green which spread away without tree or hillock to the straight edge of the horizon. White, towering clouds went blowing past overhead, their shadows on the ground seeming to follow the rippling of the grass. He sat down upon the turf, close-cropped here where deer had grazed. Thus he remained for a long time, his chin on his hand, his elbow on his knee, his eyes looking afar over that immeasurably wide landscape.

This also was one of the possessions of that green empire of Louisiana, of which the lonely man upon the island had spoken as the King of Spain's daughter. A princess she truly was with all that wealth of fertile acres. There were great, bare mountains at the far edge of them, so he had been told, where was said to lie a fabulous treasure of gold and silver. With her mines and her forests and her endlessly moving waters, this Louisiana was a regal province indeed. It was strange to him, sitting there at the edge of that enormous wilderness, to think that he and Stuart and Mr. Barton Howland might after all prove to be the means of including the last valuable miles within the boundaries of that broad realm. If that man on the island were right, it might be as a result of their effort that Louisiana should reach out so far as Grandfather's hill above the river, where through those long years had grown and flourished Grandfather's great walnut tree.

He was so lost in dreams that he had not paid much attention to Stuart who had cast himself down upon the grass beside him. But when Chris Dahlberg's far thoughts came finally wandering back again, he looked down at his friend and began to notice how worn and tired was Stuart's face, and how heavy was the cloud which brooded over it. Chris felt that he could not fathom the depths of Stuart's restlessness and of his overwhelming desire for something new. His own discouragement was so near to despair that he felt he had nothing left to offer. He turned about to look at the river, at the long bar and the great single tree which dominated it. The raft looked little at that distance, a frail toy smashed by man's arrogant carelessness against the giant hostility of nature.

Chris was a boy whose very character, even as Pierre Dumenille had seen, demanded that, when he began a task, he must pursue it to an end. But here the end seemed utterly impossible, not merely the recovery of all the logs, but the restoring of discipline and courage, of bringing back the whole wrecked venture into something which might be called success. He had almost forgotten that phase of the undertaking which was to turn the timber into money for him and for Alexis Dahlberg. It was the keeping of his word to himself, to Grandfather, to Pierre Dumenille that was the only purpose of which he had any thought now. If he failed, would he ever have real confidence again? Would not any enterprise into which he flung his energy always have behind it that whisper of doubt and the remembrance of disaster at Lone Tree Crossing?

As for Stuart and what he could be thinking, that Chris could make no attempt to guess. His comrade still lay full length upon the grass looking moodily down at the river. What would be the effect on his unstable nature if they should give up this thing? Stuart

Swift Rivers

had promised both himself and Pierre Dumenille that he would, for the first time, carry long labor to completion. His own problem was so heavy that Chris could make no effort to judge that of his friend. Yet the suspense of uncertainty was so great that the younger boy felt he could not endure it. It was surely better to face the question courageously and settle it.

"Stuart," he said, trying to keep any real expression from his tone, "Stuart, do you think that what the river men told us was right, and that we can never make this wreck float again? Do you think we ought to give it up?"

His friend did not answer for such a long time, that Chris turned finally to follow his eyes, to see if there were anything in that widespread scene below them which could so greatly absorb him. Stuart's glance was fixed upon an upper bend, where there was slowly coming into view another raft. It advanced deliberately and floated toward them at the crawling pace belonging to that manner of craft. Both the boys watched it in tense silence as it approached. Stuart spoke, finally, but in the most casual of tones:

"It's probably the last one that will go by this summer. The season for starting them downstream is well over by now."

They continued to watch as it came near. There was

time, ample time, for them to go down the path, push off their boat and row out to ask for passage to St. Louis. After all, was not that broken thing on the sand bar a failure beyond hope of remedy? Had they not given to it all that was in them, to no avail? The minutes went by one by one.

"Stuart," Chris said again, "are you going?"

A quiver went over Stuart's white face. It looked much as it had on that night in the log hut beside the river, when he had escaped with such difficulty from the evil company into which his wandering adventures had brought him. Perhaps he was thinking of that moment now. At last he spoke — one word which dropped on the still air as sharp and sudden as a pistol shot.

"No!"

There was a little pause after that one brief and decisive statement. Then Stuart spoke again more casually: "No, I am not going. Are you?"

He looked up at his companion, a slow smile spreading over his drawn face, while Chris, in his turn, relaxed into relieved and joyful reply:

"No, I am not going either."

They both got up and went closer to the edge of the bluff. The raft was so near that they could make out, in the stern, a man with a bandaged head, who might be Spike Ellerby. They were both most anxious to see whether or not the raft was to stop; and, if so, what would be the effect upon their dejected and idle crew.

But the pilot was evidently in haste to be down the river and made no motion to check his course. They could see him put his hands to his mouth to shout across to Ned Kelly, probably with the offer of help which every river man is bound to give to another. Ned Kelly's reply was brief, although the men about him were all lining up along the edge of the sandbar. Perhaps the other was too wise to offer opportunity to deserters, and felt that the best way that he could stand by a brother pilot was to sail past at a distance. The dark shape of the moving raft began presently to drift into the curve of the river and at last slowly disappeared.

Stuart, with a changed and cheerful face, strolled away along the shoulder of the bluff. In the woods below, on their own side of the river, was the far-off sparkle of water, here and there — the Indians' creek. With his eyes upon it he observed easily:

"It's not going to be so long until dark, now."

They waited, with what patience they could, until evening had passed into a night of stars without any moon. They descended the hill, got into their boat and rowed down the river, keeping to the deep black shadow cast by the bluff, in which practically all things were invisible. They pulled, this time, to the very mouth of the creek, with such gently dipping oars that the soft splash could not possibly have been heard above the murmur of water slipping over the lime-stone ledges. Once more they beached the boat, well under cover, beneath an overhanging bank, and made the rest of their way forward on foot.

They could see a low ridge at some distance from the shore, beyond which the lodges stood black against the stars, and where the camp fires were burning. All the warriors were standing about the blaze, gesticulat-ing and talking, and filling the air with noise and laughter. The boys lay in the low underbrush close to the water, and could not see the stolen logs, but could still hear them knocking together as they floated in a crowded mass at the bend of the stream just below the stony bank.

The village grew quiet as the evening advanced, and the fires subsided into heaps of glowing coals. More than once, a brave passed down to the river and came back, showing that the Indians were keeping close watch over the stolen property. When the lodges at last became silent, two men walked down together, talking as they came. They established themselves comfortably on a stretch of grass near to the high bank and above where the logs lay. Red men are not usually watchful at night, since enemies of their own kind are seldom prone to come upon them in the dark. But where they have to do with things concerning the whites, they realize that the same customs do not prevail. One Indian is seldom willing to watch alone, however. The darkness holds terror for superstitious souls who picture the night as filled with dreaded spirits and with forces which they do not understand. If the logs were to be guarded, it must be by two men together.

The boys, still lying in their place of concealment, could see the pair settling themselves for the long vigil. The Indians talked together for a little, then fell silent. Finally one of them began to nod, but was peremptorily awakened by the other.

"What are they doing now?" Stuart whispered close to Chris' ear. The two sentinels were neither talking nor sleeping, but were making odd motions with their hands just above the surface of the ground. They had built a tiny fire, for the sake of its light, a mere glow of coals in the hot darkness. One of them lifted something whose shape was difficult to make out in the dim illumination. After long puzzling, however, Chris was able to breathe a reply into the ear of his companion:

Lone Tree Crossing

"It was a moccasin he held up. They're playing the moccasin game. They're gambling."

Indians love games of chance and, in the hours when there is no pressure of work upon them, they will gamble interminably with an absorption that even a white man can scarcely understand. A certain game is a favorite with a large number of tribes; so that Chris had seen it followed amongst the Chippewa and recognized it again as these two warriors fell to playing it. It is very simple. Three moccasins are laid out in a row; one Indian takes a bullet or a stone in his hand and passes it in and out of the moccasins. He leaves it in one, and the other attempts to guess where it is. That is all.

No white man would spend a long night over such a pastime, growing more and more interested and excited with every turn. Indians are like children in their enjoyment of simple pleasures; they are like the wisest of old men in the wit and craft which they can bring to the pursuit of them. The two who were playing were evenly matched; and luck seemed to reside first with one and then with the other. The game waxed hot, and all thought of tedium or of terror of the dark was plainly at an end.

The two warriors might perhaps have heard a soft rustle now and then amongst the bushes, as though a raccoon or a weasel were stealing down to the river to drink. But such small, furry game interested them not at all while that fascinating occupation still went forward between them. The little light of their fire made the darkness like a wall all about them. They might have heard, once in a while, a gentle splash or a subdued thump as though one floating body had jostled another in the quiet course downstream, but all such gentle noises, merging into the whisper of the water, fell upon deaf ears. The bullet went in and out of the moccasins; and the fateful question of where it lay obscured all other matters.

As for the two boys, of all the toiling hours which had demanded patience and self-restraint, these asked for the most. Chris, waist deep in the gently moving stream and hidden by the shadow of the overhanging bank, laid hands upon one log after another. With the gentlest of motions he pushed them in single file across the shingle bar and within the reach of the stronger current. Some yards farther downstream Stuart was stationed, armed with the iron-hooked peavey which had been left in the boat and which he had gone back to fetch for this new adventure in log running. Just here, the water poured over a ledge in a brief stretch of rapid current. As the dark trunks came sailing slowly toward him, he gave them another impetus over the drop in the stream bed, pushing with stronger force than Chris had dared to do, but taking infinite pains that no sudden movement or unwary splash should betray what was going forward.

The water ran somewhat quicker near the mouth of the creek and carried the logs faithfully down toward the Mississippi. Half of them were dispatched . . . two thirds . . . they were nearly all gone. Chris, as absorbed as those two gamblers on the bank, pushed the last into the main channel, one, two, three. There was only one left, the great walnut tree. It was aground, of that he felt sure. But the last thing which ever would have occurred to him was the thought of leaving it as a prize for the Indians.

He waded toward it, moving as softly as he could. He looked over his shoulder and saw one of the Indians get up. Immediately he froze to complete stillness and held his breath. No, he had not been seen, the Indian was simply going back to the camp, perhaps to get food. The one who was left had stooped to blow upon the fire, anxious for more light if he were to be left alone. If the flame were to blaze high, he would catch sight of the boy in the water.

Chris was beside the log; he had pushed it free; it was floating. He let it slide past him, then slipped along on the far side of it to give it further impetus.

It grazed the bottom, floated, and grounded again. Chris could see the flare of the fire, leaping up beyond the great mass of the log; he heard a sound of feet on the shore, but dared not look about or lift himself to glance over the top of the great trunk. Now they were in deep water again, the log was floating and he was swimming beside it with his hand on the spruce outriggers. A few more yards and they would drift round a bend of the stream. He raised himself in the water to strike out more boldly. At just that instant a hand with a grasp of steel seized him by the knee and dragged him under the water.

CHAPTER VII

THE YELLOW GIANT

As he choked and struggled in the muddy creek
water, Chris felt that his lungs must burst before he
could wrench himself free of the clutching arms and
the supple legs which wrapped about him and sought
to drown him. The water of the pool was churned
to yellow foam in the furious battle which went on
in grim silence between these two who had not yet
even seen each other's face. Once Chris tore himself
loose for an instant and came to the surface, to draw
a tremendous breath and catch a fleeting glimpse of
stars and of the great hulk of the walnut log towering over him. Then he went down again with that
strangling weight still clinging to his taut body.

An Indian's life of hunting, running and riding
makes him tough and nimble; yet his training is no
more rigorous than that of a boy who works early
and late upon a wilderness farm. A red man's great
strength and power is in his legs, for his arms do no
heavy labor and are less developed than his thighs

and tremendously powerful knees. But a farmer's lad toils with every muscle of his body, day after day and year after year. He becomes hard as iron and, with his wits to help him, is a match for any other dweller in the wilderness whether it be a steel-pawed bear, a blindly infuriated bull moose, or a more human adversary. Every swing of the long scythe with which Chris had cut the grain in Nels Anderson's fields had toughened the fibre of his strong, young body and stood him now in good stead in this desperate extremity.

Again he came to the surface, and could at last see the dark tense face of his enemy emerge from the water not two feet away. They caught deep sobbing breaths, the two of them, but neither cried out. Chris could have called to Stuart for aid; but his shout would have brought the whole Indian village to the rescue of their comrade. Why the other did not lift his voice to summon his friends was a matter upon which the boy wasted no thought. It was probable that, having let the logs slip away under his very eyes, he had no wish to bring his companions to witness his undoing. He must get them back alone, or lose them utterly. To an Indian, nothing is so terrible as humiliation before his brother warriors. He will gladly perish rather than endure that.

The Yellow Giant

As the pair struggled in the water, they drifted slowly with the stream, the big walnut tree moving serenely beside them. At one moment Chris had caught one of the spruce trunks alongside it and dragged himself head and shoulders out of the water; but the great mass careened, and plunged him under again. The boy could feel the tug of the current as the force of the creek began to strengthen. He had clutched his enemy now about his slippery, naked body and was attempting, in his turn, to force him downward, but with no other result than that he went plunging, himself, to the very bottom of the pool. Now they had come to a shallow bar, where both could set their feet upon the ground. Here was waged a panting, wrestling battle, first one getting the mastery, and then the other.

Suddenly Chris heard a shout on the bank behind them. The second Indian had returned and was calling to his comrade. At the same moment he heard Stuart, finally attracted by the distant sounds of struggle in the water, come running and splashing up the margin of the stream. Chris made one tremendous effort to thrust the Indian below the surface, then gave ground a little and found that he was standing in water scarcely up to his knees, with hard stone, instead of mud, under his feet. He had come to the ledge over which the current poured swiftly to plunge into the pool below. He was still crushing the ribs of his foe in merciless embrace, but the Indian was forcing him back — backward — The rapid water snatched at such insecure footing as he could find.

He was thrust one pace farther; his feet fumbled for a purchase and found nothing as he went backward over the ledge. At the same instant he saw the vast log catch and swing on the verge of the fall, then rear up, tremendous and staggering in the pouring current. It rolled over sideways, and came crashing down into the deep pool. It scarcely more than brushed against Chris, yet the impetus of its fall was so great that it flung him outward, clear of the rocks and ledges, into still water. He came to the surface, swimming dizzily, drawing great gasps of grateful breath as his empty lungs filled. Something moved heavily under the water, and touched his knee. It was the inert body of the Indian, who had been struck fairly by the wallowing log and knocked into insensibility.

Chris dragged him to the margin of the pool, where Stuart was already wading waist-deep to meet him. His friend asked no questions, but added his

The Yellow Giant

aid to the exhausted effort Chris was making to draw his enemy from the water.

"He's still breathing," pronounced Stuart, stooping down to lay his ear to the man's chest. They left him, sprawled upon the mud, half in and half out of the water. Down the stream the walnut tree was sailing in slow majesty after the rest of the lost timbers, to join them as they rolled and jostled their way to the mouth of the creek.

Since no pursuit followed, it might be surmised that a startled brave rushed into the Indian encampment to declare that the spirits of the river had desired the white men to keep their property after all, and had laid violent hands upon one of the watchers. The Mississippi had taken back the tempting prize which they had sought to make their own. Of a bullet and three moccasins there was probably nothing said.

The men on the raft, sleeping uneasily in the smother of the hot night, were aroused before dawn by the boys' shout alongside:

"Turn out to help us. The logs are in the river." They jumped up, and came to the edge of the water, a blinking and astounded company.

"We thought you'd left us for good," declared

217

Ned Kelly, "and gone downstream with the raft that went by yesterday. Except for taking our boat, you would have been in your rights if you had. We owned it amongst us last night, that you'd done more than any of the rest of us, and that you'd had more to make you lose heart."

More than a mile downstream, a new boom was laid out from shore, and behind it the fugitive wealth of Chris Dahlberg and Shreve McCloud was finally gathered. Activities were transferred from the sandbar to the place where the logs had been caught and here they were bored, bolted and bound once more into a new brail to lie under armed guard and to be picked up when the rest of the raft should be once more afloat. Axes and hammers were wielded with a will, as the last of the frames were set together.

On Lone Tree Bar, the whole broken section of the raft, lying at the edge of the water, had now been cut free. The floating timbers were once more set in orderly array, butt to butt within the new framework, just as they had been before they met with misadventure. There remained, now, only the stranded bow portion of the raft, which the first impact had pushed high up on the bar, to be buried, unbroken in the soft sand. This must somehow be dragged free. The moment had arrived for following

The Yellow Giant

Pierre Dumenille's detailed description of "putting down a dead man."

The relief of knowing that the labor of reconstruction was in its last phase had seemed to work a miracle among the men. The shovels flew as the deep trench was dug on the shore, a hundred feet above the bar. A big trunk of slippery elm was cut down and laid at the bottom. They could not spare a single one out of the number of the stamped and measured logs which they had worked so hard to save. The green, coarse wood of the elm would serve their purpose just as well. A strong line was fastened about the center of the trunk, while all along the trench crossed stakes were laid, resting against the rough bark of the tree. Then the heavy sand was shoveled in and piled in a heap above it.

"If you pull that out, the whole bottom of the river ought to come up with it," Jacob Woolf declared. Chris, used to the hard granite of his own valley, could scarcely be convinced of the staying power of shifting sand. But presently he was obliged to believe the evidence of his own eyes.

The long, heavy line was carried over to the crosspiece of the raft which lay so deeply settled in the sand that it seemed it must rest on the bar forever. Four windlasses were connected by smaller lines to the big hawser, and the slow labor of winding up began. The sun was clear and merciless, as though even this last effort must be made as difficult as possible, as though heat and toil were bound to pursue the venture to the very end.

There were three men at each windlass, struggling and sweating, and forcing the heavy handle round and round. The ropes squeaked and tightened, the timbers began to groan.

Once, a clumsy fellow missed his hold; his rope unwound and the handle spun in murderous fury, threatening destruction to everything near. But that was a mishap long familiar to river hands. The three windlass men all sprang clear the instant that the slipping of the line gave them warning. Amidst the cheerful jeers of their comrades, they bent to their work again and wound up their rope to an even tautness with the rest. Once more the heavy log frames complained aloud as the terrific strain grew heavier and heavier. There was a strange quiver under the workers' feet, a soft, gigantic sucking sound, and all of a sudden the whole mass of timber was floating easily upon the ripples which washed Lone Tree Bar.

A shout went up, followed by relieved, almost hysterical laughter. Ned Kelly's crew had accomplished what seemed the utterly impossible. There were no words of congratulation offered either to the pilot or to those two helpers whose aid had been so great. The custom of the river did not permit any effusion of feeling, no matter what the occasion. But the face of the young Irishman who had brought the craft aground upon the bar and who now saw it afloat again, was a thing long to be remembered. Joy shone upon that homely countenance with brightness to warm the heart of any man.

"I never thought to see it," he said to the two boys who stood beside him. "You — " his voice came very near to breaking, "you can't know what it will mean to me to take her into St. Louis after all."

It was after they were fairly launched and actually moving down with the current, that Ned Kelly added a last word to Chris: "I always wanted to tell you what I felt about — about them logs being yours. But — I never could find any words for it — I knew you would come to understand some time."

The boy nodded. He did understand, now.

The last strip was picked up; the whole great structure was firmly lashed together and the voyage southward was finally begun. It seemed that luck had decided to make common cause with them at last; for the heat lifted and a cool wind blew straight downstream to waft them onward. A few skulking Indians had peered out at them as they picked up the recovered brail of logs, those straight pine stems, those rich red cedar logs which would have made such glorious canoes, that fabulously big trunk of walnut. But the red men made no offer to recapture what had once seemed so safe in their own hands. They appeared to believe that the will of the great river had decided the matter otherwise.

One hazard still lay before them, a totally unexpected one. As they came round a bend, borne by both current and wind, there appeared before them a little island, softly covered with new willow growth. Ned Kelly stared at it in amazement.

"That island wasn't there last season!" he declared.

The current and the channel swerved here and set almost directly across the river, so that the raft must turn also and make the long crossing from bank to bank, and at right angles to the wind. They moved forward easily, rocking, the short waves running under the raft and showing their undulations from one side to the other. Chris saw Ned Kelly's face grow anxious. The man was upon his mettle now, if ever he was to be in his life. Nevertheless it was

The Yellow Giant

suddenly plain that they were drifting down upon the island. The great length of the raft was halfway past the little dot of land. The wind freshened all at once in a fitful puff. Down they slipped, nearer and nearer. It seemed that the long slender line of the raft would be snapped across the head of the island as a stick is snapped across a man's knee. Chris saw Kelly's hand quiver on the steering sweep; but he gave no order to the men to swing the great oars.

"Steady on, Cap," he heard Con O'Blennes whisper. "The current's carrying us faster than the wind."

A long, agonizing minute and they were past, with the rear corner of the raft cutting a groove in the sand at the point of the island. If Ned Kelly had tried to swing his great craft, he would have plunged it to irreparable destruction.

"It was the current that saved us," Con O'Blennes remarked when they were safely by. "It's a brave man, Ned, that can just leave it to the river when he has to. The river can do you a good turn as well as a bad one."

"But," Ned Kelly repeated indignantly when the speck of green was well behind them, "but I tell you that island wasn't there last year."

"Nor won't be next year, most likely," returned O'Blennes. "It will be just washed away, to form again somewhere else. It's only one of the little tricks the river likes to play, to teach young pilots their business."

Ned Kelly reddened, but took the joke in good part.

"You'll be running a raft yourself some day, Con," he declared, but the cheerful cook shook his head.

"Not me," he said with feeling. "Let the river have her ways and me have mine. I'll take no responsibility when I'm traveling along with the Mississippi."

Other difficulties there were of bars and crossings, but for the most part the channel grew ever wider and deeper. There seemed nothing to do now but to wait and float, to float and wait as the days went by. As they slid steadily southward, Chris began to have some strange misgivings. His enterprise had passed many dangers; could he not perhaps believe that the little green-tufted island had been the last menace of which he need be afraid? The enmity of Uncle Nels, the narrow shallows of the Goose Wing, the brawling rapids of the Mississippi, the human hazard of quarrels and inexperience and loss of heart, were not all these enough? But now there must lie before him the new experience and the new risk of bringing his wares to market.

He would come to a city now, to crowding men, to many people speaking together, telling him things he might not understand, asking him questions which he might not be able to answer. What did he know of cities, he who was used only to hills and green solitudes? What could he make of any transaction which had to do with money, when he had scarcely possessed any in the whole of his life? These insistent questions began to haunt him waking and sleeping. Instead of wishing that the raft would float faster, as he had up to that moment, he began to long for the journey to go on interminably.

When he slept in the little loft in his uncle's farmhouse, his mattress was stuffed with hay from the high meadow so that, as he stirred in his sleep, the fragrance of sweet fern and dried wild herbs would come through his dreams. He would dream of that fragrance now, and think that he was at home in the breezy loft. He would dream of the stillness in the meadow and the little gray chipmunk rattling cherry stones deep inside the stone wall. He would wake with something like terror to find himself on the hard boards of the raft platform, still moving inexorably toward St. Louis.

He and Stuart talked together in the evening watches of what might be before them. Stuart seemed no more at ease than did Chris.

"I had pictured myself coming down toward St. Louis with all my pockets stuffed full of gold," the older boy said ruefully. "Yet all the gold I ever won was just those pebbles that we left behind in that hut in the woods."

He seemed to be thinking, as he spoke, of that desperate period when he had fallen to the lowest depths of his misguided adventuring.

"Do you think I will ever be able to amount to anything, Chris?" he asked with despair in his voice.

"You didn't give up at Lone Tree Crossing," his friend replied simply. Chris could see that the shoulders of the other squared a little and that his face lightened. Yes, that was a good memory. He had, once at least, refused to leave a task which proved a very hard one.

"But I have no idea what I should do now," Stuart said.

Small mischances, which are part of every expedition, never seemed to come to an end. A rope

The Yellow Giant

parted, kicking back like a vicious horse, with the result that almost immediately the long, straight outline of the raft began to warp and buckle. Ned Kelly was obliged to bring his flotilla to shore while the damage was repaired.

"It was an old line, but I think we can splice it," he said.

At the place where they had stopped there were a few houses, with a rough trail mounting the bank and going out of sight. A cluster of roofs, showing beyond the turn of the way, indicated that there was a small settlement a little distance from the shore. A well-traveled road seemed to run behind the ridge; for more than once, as they labored at the water's edge, they heard the rumble of the wheels of passing carts.

Their presence attracted a little crowd of onlookers, one or two young farmers, several fishermen who had been dabbling for catfish, and a world of variously spotted hound dogs. Talk went on from shore to raft as the work went forward.

The settlement, it appeared, was a way station on rather an important highway, the north and south road which paralleled the river. Travel through this whole immense region was, for the most part, by water. All the way downstream, however, there was,

Swift Rivers

in the north a little-used trail, farther south a more and more well-beaten track.

A little buzzing of excitement could be heard amongst the spectators; for an event had occurred a few days before which had broken abruptly into the monotony of their ordinary lives. They were glad to have some one to whom to relate it anew.

A traveler coming down from the north had stopped at the tavern. He had evidently ridden from afar, was well-mounted, and well-dressed to a certain degree. "Not just first-class, mind you, but neat appearing," one of the fishermen explained carefully. The stranger had fallen into talk with the men who dropped in at the tavern, and John Rawlins, a prosperous farmer from "up the road a piece," had struck up quite an acquaintance with him.

"Anybody might have taken up with him. The fellow was as pleasant spoken as you could have wanted to hear. Talked sort of light and quick, and had a lot of interesting kinds of things to tell," so another recounted.

The result of the evening's talk, during which Rawlins had been a little too boastful about the amount of his savings from the sale of last year's crop, was what any one might have guessed. The farmer had been roused in the night by the collie

228

dog's barking, but he awoke just too late. The familiar hiding place for money, under a brick of the hearth, had been found and rifled, and a slight figure faintly visible in the starlight was making retreat toward the gate. The furious onset of the dog and Rawlins' prompt bringing of his shotgun to bear had accomplished this much at least, that the rascal was obliged to run for his life into the woods and was not able to get back to his horse in the road.

The line had been mended and was now being wound up by slow turns of the windlass, *creak, creak*. The story went on through the sound.

"So Rawlins has the horse. It was a good one once, I expect, but it has been used so hard and fed so poorly that it's not much account now. The saddle is worth something though; it is dark brown leather with carved work around the pommel and with silver-plated stirrups."

Stuart, near the shore, flung up his head suddenly. "What was that?" he asked. "What sort of a saddle?"

The man on shore repeated and added:

"A slim, well-built critter the horse is, black, with a white stocking on his nigh foreleg. But just about dead beat when the fellow left him."

Swift Rivers

The youth swung about on the stringpiece of the raft.

"It's Pharaoh," he cried to Chris and with one leap was ashore. He vanished up the bank leaving his informant staring and speechless.

Chris went aft to speak to Ned Kelly. "I'll have to go after him," he said. There was no time to make explanation. "You must wait, wait until we come back." Ned Kelly was astonished and none too pleased, but he was allowed no time to object.

The boy hurried up the slope and came out upon the road, rough, rutted and dusty in the heat. A cart was vanishing around a turn; it was evident that Stuart had begged a ride from its owner. Hot, but doggedly determined, Chris set out to follow. He walked a long way, having time to think, as he trudged forward, that it was not so surprising that Stuart's old acquaintance, Tom Loomis, should thus reappear. He had fallen out with that companion whom Eric Knudson had discovered struck over the head in the cabin beside the river. With one of the two in the hands of justice, it would be necessary for the other to flee the North country. Evidently he had still so coveted Pharaoh that he had found time and opportunity to lay hands upon him before leaving the neighborhood.

The Yellow Giant

As he tramped over the ruts, Chris was clearly certain which of the two lawbreakers he could thank for that nick in his scythe handle. Loomis had traveled south, since St. Louis was the ultimate goal for any person who had money to spend. He had overreached himself in the matter of John Rawlins, since he who was a little too ready with his confidence was also ready with his charge of buckshot. How long ago had this happened — three days, didn't some one say? The fugitive was probably a hundred miles away by now.

He came to a gate where the cart, which had rumbled ahead of him, was still drawn up and the driver staring up the lane.

"That young fellow seemed in a right smart of a hurry," he grinned and was answered by seeing another young fellow in quite as great a hurry push past him and hasten toward the house.

It was good to see the big, comfortable white-painted dwelling, after all the huts and rude shacks which made up so many of the riverside settlements. The house was low and broad in the eaves, with a group of wide barns and sheds behind it. Although it was modeled very differently from the steep-roofed buildings of Nels Anderson's hillside farm, it stood for the same things, home, comfort, and some measure of prosperity. It gladdened the heart of Chris Dahlberg just to look at it as he came up the lane.

John Rawlins, the owner of the place, was broad also and had a look of comfortable peace about him, although at the moment of the boy's appearance he was in a state highly overwrought. Stuart had been, it was quite true, in such headlong haste that he had taken very little time to explain anything. Beyond the big barn, in a fenced paddock, a black horse was grazing, a horse which could be, indeed, none other than Pharaoh. The sight of him had so excited his former master that the youth seemed able to do nothing but repeat breathlessly that the animal was his and that he must have him.

"Yes," Rawlins was saying, with loud irony, as Chris came near. "I suppose he is your horse — maybe. You just lent him to a friend, I take it, and the friend went off in such a hurry that he had to leave his mount behind him. I don't think much of your friends, young sir. I've had enough to do with rogues just now to last me for a good space of time."

Chris came up beside his comrade and spoke quietly. "We know all about the man who left him. He had stolen the horse after Stuart had sold him. And the fellow had a shot at each of us, trying to get the horse earlier."

The Yellow Giant

Rawlins' angry loudness of tone dropped a little. "Now that's talk that I understand better," he said. "But," to Stuart, "have you any proof to offer that the beast is really yours?"

Stuart pursed his lips and whistled. The grazing Pharaoh lifted his head and pricked his ears. As the boy whistled again, the horse wheeled about and cantered toward the fence. In one easy leap he was over it and had come galloping across the grass to push his nose into his master's hand.

"I reckon he's yours," admitted Rawlins. He had been moved, as Chris had been, by the beautiful lightness of that jump, and by the evident joy of reunion between lad and horse. "I don't wonder you're glad to get him back. Well, I won't keep him from you. I don't receive stolen goods, even though I have lost my money in exchange."

"Oh, I'll buy him from you," Stuart offered eagerly. After a moment of thought he was obliged to amend his offer. "I haven't got any money now, but I feel sure that I can earn some in St. Louis. If you like — " he faltered, but went on courageously. "Perhaps it would be more honest if I left him here with you and came to get him when I had enough to pay you."

"No," said Rawlins. "I don't care to sell a horse

that isn't mine. The fellow from whom he was stolen in the first place is the one who should have the money. But as you haven't any, young man, we won't need to say too much about that. Just take the horse and go along with you. You'll find the saddle and bridle on a peg just inside the barn door."

As Stuart, completely radiant, ran to gather the rest of his property, John Rawlins turned to Chris. "You seem to have a little steadier head than the other one; can you tell me a bit more about this?"

Chris began to tell him. There was something of the same honest heartiness in Rawlins that he had felt and understood in Shreve McCloud. It invited confidence in spite of the fact that the man could not forbear breaking in often. The two of them were presently sitting on a bench under the grapevine, while the account had lengthened to embrace Nels Anderson, the high meadow and the adventure of log running. Rawlins interrupted many times, but finally seemed to get the gist of the whole story.

It must have been twenty minutes later that Stuart came out of the barn. He had taken time to brush the horse's coat until it glistened. The poor animal was worn and thin and had been ill cared for, but he had the same spirited stride, the same fine arch of the neck. The face of Stuart Hale was a glory of bright happiness.

"I will have to ride him to St. Louis, now," he said to Chris. "You won't really need me on the raft, since the going is so much easier. Will you mind it if I go on with Pharaoh, and meet you in the town? We will surely find you, some way."

Chris agreed that he did not mind, whereat Stuart mounted immediately, and was off through the gate. He looked back once to wave his hand in farewell. It was upon seeing that backward glance that Rawlins suddenly smote his great hand upon his thigh.

"Why," he roared, "how didn't I think of it before? That's the boy Tom Loomis was asking for. That's the very boy!"

He collected himself enough to make the matter a little clearer. "You see I'm a talker," he confessed, "a good deal of a talker, and that smart rogue Loomis down at the tavern got me going and telling all about myself. I can't blame your young friend here for not showing much wisdom when he met those rogues up north, because I showed even less. But I remember now that the man kept putting in questions that didn't have to do with me and where I kept my fool money; he asked once or twice about a boy, black haired and tall. Said the lad was going down the river, and wanted to know if he had passed. He insisted that he was bound to catch him up somewhere. He declared that he had some pretty important business with the fellow and that he would follow him far to complete it. I think he let drop that the affair had something to do with gold. Do you know anything about gold being mixed up with these strange matters?"

Yes, Chris could tell him about the gold also, gold over which the evil partners had quarreled with murderous ferocity, gold which turned out to be worth nothing. It was plain that Loomis felt that he had a score to settle with Stuart Hale. "But," the boy cried out, breaking off in the anguish of a sudden idea, "there is Stuart riding off alone toward St. Louis and that man, who wants to do him mischief, is on the road somewhere, and still looking for him."

"I don't believe they will find each other," returned Rawlins grimly. "The rascal got away, but we know he didn't get far. There's some of the neighbors around here have been helping me to search for him. We have all been taking turns keeping up the hunt. It is certain that he is somewhere in that great stretch of forest south of the town, along beside the river. We've got our posse spread all through the wood so I don't think he can slip through our fingers.

The Yellow Giant

There's a good stout jail in this county; and I think he'll lodge inside of it before so very many days are out. I'm even counting on getting my money back."

Chris got up and moved toward the gate. He must return to the raft if they were to get forward before night. No matter what might be his anxiety concerning Stuart, he could not follow him on foot or send warning after him. Rawlins walked a little distance with him.

"The lad has a good horse — and a good friend," he observed simply. "He can show it a little more, how he loves his horse, than how he loves his friend."

If Chris had felt a little sore dismay that Stuart was to leave him just now, when his own misgivings for the future were growing great, the farmer's downright words were of much comfort to him. It was true that Stuart's presence on the raft was no longer really necessary. With the final achievement at Lone Tree Crossing, the actual battle against the river was won. But Chris would miss him, of that the younger boy was very conscious as he said good-bye to the farmer and tramped away.

Ned Kelly was fretting to be gone and asked few questions about the nonappearance of Stuart, so in haste was he to cast off and put out into the current. The pilot was watching the mended break in the rope too anxiously to have time to hearken to the tale Chris was recounting to Con O'Blennes and Jacob Woolf. As daylight waned, they were drifting past a bar which showed ghostly white in the twilight. Of a sudden a man appeared out of the woods to run over the sand and send a call across the water.

"I believe he wants us to pick him up," said Ned Kelly, whose ears were quicker than those of the others. "At least we'll send the boat in and make sure of what he's asking."

Jacob Woolf and Chris got out the skiff and pulled inshore. The solitary figure stood waiting, and looking back, now and again, toward the forest from which it had emerged. Chris rowed slowly and warily. This might be one of the searching posse, asking if they had seen the fugitive. Or might it not be — some one else?

The nose of the boat had almost touched the sand when the man came hastening toward them. There were noises of crashing and shouting among the trees on the shore above, as though people were moving through the underbrush, to close in upon the fugitive on the sandbar. He came wading out to them, knee-deep in the water. He was a smallish man, his clothes, once neat, were dirty and torn; his face was haggard with weariness and hunger. He spoke in that thin, light voice which Chris had heard before.

"Take me aboard," he panted. "I'll pay you well. I have important business in St. Louis. Just get me on board."

Chris dipped the oars sharply as he backed water, away from the bar.

"No," he shouted across the widening space between them.

Jacob Woolf's booming voice repeated the refusal. "We don't carry passengers of your kind, Tom Loomis."

They had reached the raft and were moving downstream again when they saw the group of men break through the trees and advance across the sand. Loomis ran to the very point of the bar and shouted a final despairing plea to the raft as it drifted away. Jacob Woolf was looking back at him, as he and Chris bestowed the boat in its place on the stern platform.

"That man is going to lodge in the county jail tonight. But I wouldn't be surprised if he got a little ducking, first, from those friends of John Rawlins'. They're closing in on him in a way that looks like no nonsense."

The next day progress was once more interrupted

by a second parting of the damaged rope. It was plain that there was nothing to do but discard it entirely and string a new line. A long, tedious process it was, delaying them a good twenty-four hours. Every one was vexed and impatient with the mishap, every one on board except Chris.

"I wonder you don't take it like the rest of us," Con O'Blennes said to the boy curiously. "You don't seem to care now whether we ever get to St. Louis."

Chris scarcely replied. Without Stuart beside him, the unknown difficulties of the future seemed more appalling than ever. No, he felt that he cared very little whether or not they made haste to reach their journey's end.

One morning Ned Kelly, standing near him, pointed to a low green bluff rising at a distance above the flat shore.

"Keep your eyes on that, and you will see something presently."

Chris waited and watched as the hill came nearer, not understanding what it could be that he was to expect. He did not know until they had rounded the turn just below the bluff.

"Your first sight of the Missouri is something to remember," Con O'Blennes said at his elbow.

He was right. One does not often see one smooth,

The Yellow Giant

clear Titan of a river joined by another, a tumbling, tawny giant rushing out of a far broader valley and flinging a yellow flood into the translucent waters of the first stream. It is thus that the Mississippi and the Missouri meet.

As they passed and continued southward, Chris noted that, for the space of a mile or two, the dissimilar waters refused to mingle. Finally boils of mud began to come up to the surface of the clearer half, the Mississippi's; then the line of difference grew vague and wavered and at last the river rolled forward, the same muddy yellow from bank to bank. The far ranges of the Rocky Mountains are washed at their rugged bases by that cloudy stream, which brings down the silt and carries it innumerable miles to be deposited in the delta lands at the Gulf. With the inrushing of that sea of mud, the upper Mississippi, clean, broad and majestic, comes to an end. The lower river, deeper, swifter and less wide, goes forward through further adventuring to reach the sea.

For as long as they could, the crew of the raft floated in the clear portion of the stream.

"Mud is no good for logs," Ned Kelly said. "It's well that we aren't to carry this craft much farther."

There were only a few more miles of travel now.

Swift Rivers

There was a sudden sight of houses on a ridge, a big church lifting above the other buildings, and steep-roofed dwellings all about it, more than Chris had ever dreamed of in one community. The worn travelers reached the mouth of a slough, a backwater which seemed to be paved solid, from bank to bank, with floating logs, and which had a big, screaming sawmill built upon the shore. A rain of orders from Kelly guided the crew as they swung the sweeps and brought the bow of the raft across the current. Chris had forgotten all his misgivings now. He felt only that the dangers by water were over, that he had actually carried his enterprise from the foot of that far range of hills at the very borders of the country, down, down, into the heart of a new world.

They had reached their journey's end and this was St. Louis. As they came to land, Chris Dahlberg had eyes for but one thing, that Stuart Hale was standing on the shore and, furthermore, that the tremendous erect figure of Pierre Dumenille was beside him.

CHAPTER VIII

THE LITTLE NUT TREE

Stuart Hale and Chris were quarreling. In the room of their little lodging house near the shore of the river, they sat on opposite sides of the table and contended together in fierce argument. Money lay spread out on the board between them.

"It was your idea," asserted Chris, all the obstinacy of his character behind his words, "it was your idea that it would be a good venture to bring logs down to the market. Now that they are sold, this is your share."

"It is not my share," returned Stuart with heat. "You find me in the worst trouble that my foolishness has ever brought me into, you bring me along with you and you help me — " his voice faltered, but recovered as he went courageously on, "you help me see a thing through for the first time in my life. And then you talk about money. Every penny that's there you have earned, and you know in your stubborn heart that it's true. And you know besides that

243

you need it for your grandfather, if he is to be safe and comfortable; and you need it for yourself, if you ever are to get that learning that you want so much and say so little about."

"And what do you need it for?" Chris stood his ground. "You know you must begin to think what you are to do next. And whatever you decide, it can't be managed without a single penny. I know that," he concluded, "because before this I have scarcely ever had a single one of my own."

Stuart sat, uneasily silent, looking down upon the gold and the notes upon the table. "You are right in one thing," he began finally, "I begin to think — I have been thinking for a long time about what I should do now. I could go back with you up the river and help with another season of logging — "

He paused to reflect a little longer, while the delight which leaped into Chris Dahlberg's eyes at the suggestion brought a flush of color to his own face. "There haven't been many places where I was really wanted," he declared bitterly, "so it doesn't seem easy to turn away from you and Pierre Dumenille and that prince of a grandfather of yours. I feel how much I want to go along with the three of you. But — but — " he hesitated long again, "I do believe, and Dumenille believes, too, that the right way is for me to do some

244

The Little Nut Tree

thing else. I have talked with him a great deal in this time we have been waiting for you." With no effort at recollection he repeated to Chris the very words of Dumenille's advice, forceful words which neither boy was ever to forget:

" 'Stuart, I think you were fashioned by *le bon Dieu* to build things and look for things and discover things. But a man cannot properly go about that without a little learning. I know that is true, because there have been a thousand things that I would have done, except for the one difficulty that made them all impossible. A man who is the son of a wandering French trapper and a Chippewa woman, who has never seen the inside of a schoolhouse — such as he must see a hundred doors closed to him, because of what he does not know.' "

"We go up every day," Stuart went on, "to that house where the French Sisters are nursing Langford and getting him well again, and while I wait for Pierre to finish talking to him, I go over what he has said to me. He is right, I must have more learning if I am to know how mines are to be dug or roads built over mountains. I have thought of it before," he confessed frankly, "but it meant such long hard work, to study all that I needed to know, that I did not think I could hold to it as far as the end. But now," he

245

looked across at Chris with a new light in his eyes, "now I verily believe that I can. Without you and Pierre Dumenille, I would never have come to have enough confidence in myself even to try."

Chris went back, in memory, over the months of their acquaintance, and could see what Pierre Dumenille's quick eye had discerned almost immediately. Stuart was indeed a builder, a discoverer, bold and resourceful and, if he could only achieve it again, possessed of staying power enough to see a thing to success.

"I believe," declared Chris seriously, feeling that he was offering his friend the highest tribute which words could express, "I believe that you could be good at mining and building, as good as Pierre Dumenille is at being a pilot."

Stuart's decision was now definitely made, with the result that the violent difference over sharing the money came to an end. He was to return to Pennsylvania, to his own people, and was to set himself at studying again, this time with direct purpose. It was plain that he could not make the homeward journey without money, so that he consented, finally, to receive as his portion an amount barely sufficient to carry him home. It was necessary, so the practical Chris pointed out, that he and Pharaoh should eat as they traveled. Stuart was already pondering the details of the journey.

"It would be quicker to take the horse on board a steamer, if I can find one going up the Ohio. And I think there is no time to be lost."

It was his intention, if he did take a boat, to work his way; therefore the amount of money which he needed was ridiculously small. Chris was still determined that his share should be greater. In the end another compromise was made.

"You know," Stuart reminded Chris, "what John Rawlins said about the man up by the Goose Wing River who bought Pharaoh from me, and how it was he who had lost what he paid for the horse? I wanted to buy the horse from Rawlins; but instead, will you take the money to August Viborg — that was the name of the man that I sold him to? I can tell you just how to find him. Then I can know that Pharaoh really belongs to me again, when he and I set out for home."

The two boys got up abruptly and went about some small business, each of his own, as though it were dangerously pressing. If they had to part, it was not to be at once, and there was no need of talking too much of it until the day should come.

When Chris had first come to shore with the raft, and found Pierre Dumenille waiting for him, he had

not had the least idea what a person should do, who
brings timber from the far hill country to the waiting
market. But this was a matter with which Pierre was
as familiar as with the moods and currents of the
Mississippi.

He had brought Chris, next day, into the counting
room of that St. Louis merchant who owned the sawmill. There was a company gathered there, five or six
gentlemen, very impressive with their tall beaver hats,
their high stocks and strapped trousers. They seemed
to Chris, for the first moment, to be as appalling and
as numerous as though there were a score of them.
He saw upon the table a thin section of walnut, a
piece, he recognized, sawed from one of his smaller
hardwood logs. That, at least, looked familiar. His
eyes followed it when one of the strangers took it up.
To this man he was introduced by Pierre, and learned
that he was Monsieur Gervraise, from New Orleans,
a builder of ships. Chris recollected how Shreve
McCloud had spoken of this excitable acquaintance.
Would he truly weep upon the boy's shoulder, as the
Scotchman had foretold? In spite of his shyness Chris
chuckled in remembrance; the Frenchman smiled de-
lightedly in response; and they were acquainted. Monsieur Gervraise did not weep, but there was excite-

The Little Nut Tree

ment in his fine eyes as he examined the beautiful pattern of wood.

"Northern walnut," he said, "grown slowly, without too much water and without too much heat. I have seen that noble tree of yours down by the river, my dear sir, and I judge it to have had a century at least of splendid life. A year of seasoning would not be too much for it. The fairy tales tell of great things done in a year and a day; we who have to do with wood think it better, if it is a hundred years and one."

He looked about at the company, all of them interested and some of them amused at his flaming eagerness. He went on, still addressing himself chiefly to Chris:

"We have a new ship upon our ways, down beside the Gulf, the *Golden Age*. For her figurehead I have long planned there should be an embodiment of Father Time with great wings, with his hour glass and long scythe." He began to speak more quickly, as his excitement and enthusiasm rose. "I go to my best carver, a man with a true eye and a cunning hand, and tell him what I must have. 'Let the wings sweep so,' I say," — his illustrating gesture upset a beaver hat on the table and sent it rolling across the floor, but the slight mishap brought never a pause in the fluency of his speech — " 'and let the scythe be poised exactly for its proper swing.' 'I will indeed make you just that which you ask,' he assures me, 'but where do you find me a block of wood great enough for such an image? Can I make wings and scythe and mighty figure out of these poor things which the shipyard offers? You would not insult me, Monsieur Gervraise, by suggesting that I carve in sections so noble a work as that which you desire. Wings made up in pieces, sir, do you ask a master craftsman to set his hand to such a thing? Bring me as noble a block as the idea is noble, a block of perfect hardness and perfect grain. Then shall your Father Time breast the seas for generations to come.'

"I look everywhere," Monsieur Gervraise hastened on to tell them, "I seek here and I seek there, in all the places where I buy my lumber, but what do they offer me? The perfect logs are small; the big ones are coarse; I am in despair; I know not what to do. And then," he flung up his hands as he came to the dramatic climax, "then your excellent friend, Monsieur Pierre Dumenille, takes me down to the waterside and shows me, lying amongst the ripples, that of which I have only dared to dream!"

Chris, watching with fascinated eyes every rapid expression which swept over the shipbuilder's mobile face, was not sure but that the promised tears were actually not far away.

Bargains for other parcels of the lumber were made in a more prosaic manner. Each of the gentlemen there had his own needs, had looked over what Chris had brought, and found it good. One man was plainly Spanish, another spoke with a leisurely and liquid flow of words which Chris afterward learned to recognize as Virginian. None of them haggled; all of them were definite and prompt. Chris forgot to be abashed in their unfamiliar presence; he and they were there upon common ground, all of them interested in timber and what could be made from it. A long lean boy from the hill country, sunburned and a little hollow under the cheek bones, was not so greatly out of place in that carefully dressed gathering. He had that to give which they were glad to receive; and they all met upon equal footing. But he did feel a little dazed afterward when all were gone except the pleasant faced proprietor of the counting room and Pierre Dumenille. A clerk was called in with a great bag of money, and he, in a dry, matter-of-fact manner, magically transformed the bills of exchange into a heap of bank notes and heavy gold pieces.

Chris Dahlberg's first effort was to settle with Pierre Dumenille for the making and the transporting of his portion of the raft. In that undertaking he made no progress at all.

"With McCloud, yes, there may be some small matters to arrange when you pass that way again," Pierre said to him. "But with me, after you have toiled so well under my command, after you have served my dearest friend, do you think there can be any talk of stuff like this?" His scornful gesture dismissed the money as something of not the slightest account.

There remained the two letters to be attended to, that surprising missive entrusted to Chris for the mails by Mr. Barton Howland, and the other which Chris was to present, himself, when he should find out where a certain Mr. David Payne might reside. From some talk dropped in the counting room, he had learned that Mr. Payne was a minister. He and Stuart went together to the tavern by the waterside where was collected the mail to be carried up the Ohio by the next steamboat. The clerk received his letter, frankly read the address, and then looked up to stare with equally frank amazement at this tall lad in shabby raftsman's clothes who was dispatching a red sealed epistle addressed to Mr. Andrew Jackson, President of the United States.

Long after, an answer to that missive sought and

The Little Nut Tree

found Chris in his far corner of the mountain country. It offered the thanks and appreciation of the President, and declared that the suggestion of Mr. Jackson's friend, Barton Howland, had been very timely. Certain geographical vagueness in high places might indeed have set the headwaters of the Goose Wing River outside the boundaries of the Louisiana Purchase when its limits were finally determined. A veritable treasure house of grain, iron and lumber was unlocked for the people of the United States on that day when Chris and Stuart set sail southward from the mouth of the Goose Wing. But of all this Chris could know nothing, now, as he went on to ask where he should look for Mr. David Payne.

"He has a church up yonder, a few squares beyond the cathedral," the boys were told.

Chris waited until the next day, which was Sunday, to set out to find the little Protestant church, small and inconspicuous at that date amid a French Catholic community. Stuart and Pierre walked part of the distance with him; but Stuart was going to see Joe Langford on that sunny morning and Pierre Dumenille was to join the throng moving up to the doors of the great cathedral.

"That Good Friend who is making my own friend well, must not go unthanked," Pierre declared.

253

Swift Rivers

Chris went forward, almost solitary now, in the streets where the Sunday peace reigned everywhere. This must indeed be the church of Mr. David Payne, a low building with its door almost upon the street. Chris had never been in any other than the little Lutheran church which the settlers in the Goose Wing Valley had built, small and square and whitewashed, with the short solid spire of the rural churches in the Old Country.

The service here had begun, and since there was no one to bear him company in being a few moments late, Chris went in alone through the open door and sat down in the nearest narrow pew. The hymn was just ending and a man with bent shoulders and a rugged, striking profile had got up to read from the great Bible. The singing by the scanty choir had sounded rather meager, but never before had Chris heard such music as that of the great voice which went rolling through the room.

The boy was so unused to any church custom but his own, that he was obliged to pay somewhat more attention to the times of getting up and sitting down during the service than to listening to the psalms and the long prayer. He felt that eyes might be watching this rudely dressed stranger and would criticize any awkward negligence on his part in following what the

The Little Nut Tree

others did. It was with a sense of relief that he saw every one settle down, finally, to listen to the sermon. He understood about sermons. Those of the good old Pastor at home always made him feel peaceful and a little sleepy. An hour of quiet would be pleasant now. David Payne was more plainly visible as he came forward to preach. He was strongly built, not very tall, with the round shoulders of a scholar. His forehead was high; his eyebrows overshadowed deep-set, dark and burning eyes. As he began to speak, his glance ran rapidly from face to face, as though he were gathering them all together to listen to him.

It was cool and shadowy in that unadorned room with its low windows. But windows, walls, even the people about him, seemed to Chris to go far away, while the clear, brilliant light of all glorious things of the mind and spirit beat down about him. He felt that the man before him was explaining one of the most difficult truths of all religious thinking, but that his winged words and soaring images made it infinitely clear. David Payne was a master of teaching as well as of preaching. Certain sentences, which seemed to thrust themselves bodily into his sermon, made reference to the school which he was hoping to found, a project evidently so dear to his heart that he could not speak for half an hour and keep quite free of it.

Swift Rivers

For young spirits in a new country, he was saying, education was as essential as in the older communities.

"Let no one tell me," he declared, "that the eager minds which dwell in this unhampered land are not hungry for learning."

The sermon came to an end; there was a little more singing, and the audience filed out. Many of the company cast curious or friendly glances at the tall boy sitting alone in the pew beside the door. He seemed so absorbed in thoughts of his own that no one spoke to him. Chris could hear the voices outside, as the people lingered for a little exchange of Sunday morning greeting on the street without. David Payne's deep tones were audible through all the others; the minister had come round to the front of the church to speak to each of his congregation at the door. After they were all gone, perhaps Chris would muster the courage to go to him and tell him of their common friend, Mr. Barton Howland, and of the letter.

The minister's piercing eyes had not failed to notice that new face amongst his hearers, a face rapt and shining, as of one looking forth suddenly upon new worlds. When the last footstep died away, he came hastening back into the shadowy room, just as Chris rose from his place.

The Little Nut Tree

"Young man, I want to speak to you," and, "I have a letter for you." The two spoke in the same breath.

David Payne broke the seal and read slowly. He looked from the page to Chris and back again and repeated the last sentence aloud: " 'A young man apparently of intelligence and enterprise, fit material for that work which you are proposing to undertake.' "

Great matters are often settled in few words. David Payne's zeal for establishing liberal education in a new country was of the same sort and measure as Chris Dahlberg's desire to learn. The school had been commenced already, with a dozen students and with Payne himself as the sole teacher.

"But it will grow," David Payne declared, "how it will grow when I have got together all the proper things! I want young men and bricks and teachers and timbers and ideas and money, all of those things, and God will send them to me. One thing I have plenty of already, land enough for all the buildings which we shall ever need. Land in this new community is like water and air, free for any man to take according to his requirement."

It was arranged that Chris was to return to St. Louis after one more winter season of logging, and after Grandfather had been safely provided for out of the proceeds of the two ventures. Thereafter, for a few years, Chris was to spend his winters here beside the Mississippi and his summers in the north.

"And I will find just the timbers which you will need for your first building," Chris declared, glowing with a glorious enthusiasm. "I know just where there grows big white pine for columns at the door, such as they have at the cathedral yonder. And oak for rafters, the oak of northern forests, you shall have that also."

"And I shall have you," returned David Payne. "Columns and timbers, we need them, it is true, but they stand for nothing beside the living material which must go to build up that which we hope to achieve."

Thus, as has been said, a great matter was briefly brought to its conclusion.

Two days later, Chris said good-bye to Stuart Hale on the St. Louis landing — the levee, men were beginning to call it — that long ledge of rock which was to become, only a very few years later, a thronged and famous water front. Their farewells were short and somewhat gruff, as the words of such a parting were bound to be.

"I will be back with you just as soon as I can manage it, you may be certain of that," Stuart said.

Chris could not even say so much; but he wrung his

friend's hand and declared only, "We'll be waiting for you, Grandfather and I." The steamer, the Ohio River packet, a far larger vessel than any which they had seen in the course of their voyaging, rang her bell to summon lingering passengers on board. A moment later, she was backing out into the stream and Chris was left staring blankly at a spot where once had been a boat with a dark figure waving from the upper deck, but which was presently only an empty space of moving water.

Pierre Dumenille had left the two boys to exchange their good-byes alone. His own farewell to Stuart and his few words of commendation and advice had been spoken at the lodging house on the evening before. But now, by unaccountable coincidence, Dumenille's tall, lithe person came moving through the little crowd and Chris, walking silently up the bank, could feel that a good friend was walking beside him.

Chris was to travel by keel boat and was to work his way just as Stuart intended to do. The Captain had accepted his application immediately. "Shipped down with Pierre Dumenille, did you? I'll always take on a hand that's worked with him and that he recommends. He's the finest man on the river, to my way of thinking." In this pleasant agreement, the journey back to the Goose Wing River was begun.

Swift Rivers

Pierre Dumenille would be detained somewhat longer in St. Louis, on business concerning the interests of Shreve McCloud. Joe Langford's slow recovery may also have had something to do with his delay. Chris, at various times, had been to see Joe, a white spectre hovered over by the watchful Sisters, and slowly coming back to his proper strength. It was probable that he and Dumenille would fare northward together as soon as the autocratic Mother in charge would pronounce the journey possible.

Chris would have liked, on that upriver voyage, to stop at the wooded island and tell Mr. Barton Howland of the happy results following the delivery of the letter. But the toiling keel boat did not wish to check its course so that all he could do, as they moved past Howland's Island, was to watch the thin smoke going up from his friend's chimney and take it as a signal that everything was safe again in that lonely household.

Enthusiastic welcome awaited him when he landed alone at Goose Wing River. But here he tarried only long enough for a friendly talk with McCloud and the settling of all business matters. Next spring he was to drive down pine logs again; and through the winter he was to get out hard wood to be brought the length of the upper valley on sledges.

The Little Nut Tree

"We can't take whole rafts of oak and walnut down, but we'll find some way to get it to a market that keeps calling for more and more," McCloud declared. "I never really thought that you would carry that big log south; but it was well worth transporting, so they tell me. I should like to have seen the face of Gervraise when his impassioned eye first fell upon it."

When Chris set forth again, first by oars and finally, as the river became shallow, going forward on foot, he began to feel such pressing eagerness to be at his journey's end that the miles of travel appeared interminable. Yet he took time, as he trudged up the trail, to turn aside for a few hundred yards and visit once more the tumble-down hut where he and Stuart had joined their fortunes. It was probable that no one had come thither after the day when, upon Eric Knudson's information, the men of the neighborhood had come to carry away the injured desperado. There was still a pile of gray ashes on the hearth where Stuart and Chris had built their fire. He thrust his fingers through them to see if by chance either of the lumps of false gold, which they had left behind, had accidentally found concealment there. But there was nothing; it was true, then, that the smaller man of those two companions had wrested it from the other and carried it away.

Swift Rivers

Chris slept that night at the same farmhouse where Eric Knudson had applied, and learned of the final outcome of that adventure. There was no jail or magistrate within a hundred miles, but the determined farmer had harnessed his cart and driven the helpless man that whole distance to deliver him into the hands of justice.

"We found his horse tied in the woods; at least it was not his, but my neighbor Hans Schlemel's, stolen a week or two before," his host told Chris. "That was evidence enough against him, even without our knowing that the pair had been working through this region for some time, laying hands on this and that, but never completing any of the bigger robberies they must have planned. His comrade vanished, I am glad to say." He was pleased and interested to learn of the later fate of Tom Loomis.

From here, Chris sought out the house of August Viborg, one-time purchaser of Pharaoh. It took him some miles off the main road of his travel but it was an errand not to be neglected.

"The black was a good horse," Viborg said, "and I was sorry to lose him. I really only bought him because I had pity for the boy who was sick and hungry. I had some little doubts as to whether the young man was honest, and when the animal disappeared, it made me feel that I had not been mistaken. And here he has got the horse back from the thief and sends me the money again, all these hundreds of miles! Well, well, it is good to know that the lad had an honest heart, it is good indeed. You are Alexis Dahlberg's grandson, are you? We've been hearing about you and the logs you carried down. It ought to mean a deal to all of us, that you got them to market in the end. There was never a time when it did not hurt me to burn up the fine oak and pine, and to split the walnut into fence rails, while we were clearing the fields for the plough."

And now Chris was nearing home at last. He was walking the last stage of the journey up the familiar valley, where the hills were touched with the color of early autumn and the wheat fields were smooth and yellow after the harvest. Summer heat still lingered, and the day was beginning clear and warm as he came in sight of the Anderson farm.

At his last night's lodging he had told his hosts that he would be gone at the first hint of daylight, and thus it was that he came up the road toward the long roofed house and the clustering barns while the morning was still young. As he tramped forward, he thought of Pierre Dumenille and of the argument and speculation upon the raft concerning the question of whether or not their pilot would stop to speak to his former friend. As Chris had said to Stuart, he did not himself know what he should do. Nor did he know now whether or not he should enter again that place where his whole childhood had passed. It is possible that he might have gone by, but one of the farm laborers, loading a rick of straw at a loft window, looked over the gate and saw him approaching. He raised a great shout of welcome, and presently Freda came running out, bright-eyed and with hair flying, to catch Chris by the arm:

"Oh, we are so glad, so glad you have come back. Come in quickly, Chris. Surely, surely you would not pass by?"

"But my uncle — " Chris was beginning. Freda broke in upon his hesitation.

"You would never be so unforgiving as to let that matter still stand," she urged. "No, I know you forgave him when you pulled him out of the water. He is up on the hillside yonder marking trees to be cut. Ever since word came back that your log running had been such a success, he has been hoping that some day you would take timber down the river for him also."

It is probable that Nels Anderson was ashamed to face his nephew with such a request, and so remained invisible on the wooded hillside, even though a messenger must have gone hastily up the slope to tell him that Chris Dahlberg had returned. Chris himself, however he might feel should he meet his uncle face to face again, could not refuse Freda's urging, and so went in. As he sat at the familiar table and broke his long morning fast upon the feast which Freda and her mother set before him, he felt all the old rancor slip away. It was impossible to forget that timid Selma Anderson had often provoked her husband's displeasure by daring to be kind to him, and that Freda, with growing sturdiness of independence, had always taken his part. His uncle's surly authority would become less and less in that household as Freda grew older. Yes, he would take the Anderson logs to market, but it would not be for Uncle Nels.

When the bountiful meal was ended at last, he said to his cousin:

"Will you wrap that piece of honeycomb in grape leaves for me? I am going to take the trail over the mountains and I want to leave it with a friend."

Freda did as he asked, but could not restrain her curiosity. "Are you like our heathen forbears, Chris, who put out offerings for the spirits and demons of the wood to bring their good will?"

No, Chris was not just like that, though he thought

it probable that his offering would go exactly where such gifts went even in the heathen time in the Old Country a thousand years ago. But he left Freda with her guesses unanswered, and walked away up the path that crossed the hill.

Even now he must turn aside and go through the gap in the wall that surrounded the high meadow. Some one had mowed the grass; that was as it should be, for mountain hay must not go a year uncut. It was not done as evenly or as closely as he and Grandfather had been wont to mow it; that was as it should be also. It was just such a day as when he had stood there a year ago; once again it was hot in the sun, cool in the shade, with clouds sailing over the mountain tops and a dark speck swinging in the air, which was an eagle. It was exactly as he carried it in his memory and in his heart through all the miles of voyaging.

He unwrapped his package of honeycomb and set it down on a smooth sunny stone at the corner of the wall. He was quite certain that very soon after he had gone away and the sound of his departing footsteps had diminished in the distance, a small furry head would come over the wall and a yearling bear or a thin tired mother bruin would run an appreciative tongue over the sticky sweetness. Chris felt that he

The Little Nut Tree

owed the bear tribe a good turn for that night he was lost in the snow, and could think of no other means of repaying it.

He crossed the hill, descended to the highroad again and tramped steadily along the last miles. Word of his coming had somehow flown ahead of him and there were many waiting at farmhouse gates to welcome him home — Brasks and Jorgensons and Gottorps. But nowhere would he allow himself to be delayed; he was too near to his journey's end to permit of any lingering now. He left the highway at last to turn in at the door of the low-roofed dwelling of Eric Knudson.

Knudson was red with pleasure but unable to say a single word further than "So, you are back! That is good." Anna wept over Chris to his great embarrassment. But even they could not keep him after he had got an answer to his immediate question, "Is Grandfather here?"

No, Alexis Dahlberg, the moment he got word that Chris was on his journey up the valley, had insisted on going back to the cabin on the hill.

"I want to be there when he comes," was all the explanation he would give, and he had set out and would let no man go with him. Chris was out of the

Swift Rivers

door almost before Anna had finished telling him. But Knudson, with his long stride, came after him and walked a portion of the way.

"The old man will be safe from want now?" he asked. "That is what we have wished above all things might come out of the log running."

Chris set forth his plans, to rebuild and make stout and comfortable the old cabin in the forest, and to make ample provision with the Knudsons for Grandfather's safe care in the winter while he himself was away. Knudson nodded with pleasure over every item.

"That will make Anna glad, to see Alexis Dahlberg have everything a brave old man should," he said. "I never heard her lament over the little we had, and the hardship of our way of living, except when it bore heavy on your Grandfather. He grows feeble, though no one in the wide world would get him to admit it." He parted from Chris at the foot of the last climb and left the boy to go forward alone.

It seemed to Chris that he looked upon that green mountain slope with new eyes after his far journeying, that while he had thought of the river valley through every day of his absence, he had forgotten how fair it was. Had he ever noticed before the difference between the rustling sun-dappled shade of birch woods and the cool, silent blackness under the

268

shadow of the towering pines? He saw everything and yet saw nothing, for his one thought now was to hasten on. He was breathless when he reached the top of the climb.

The door of the cabin was open and Grandfather was within, making a little fire on the hearth in preparation for the evening meal. Had he aged so while Chris was gone, or had the boy forgotten this also, that Grandfather moved so slowly and that his hands were unsteady as he laid the faggots in place? It seemed that he must have heard the step on the threshold, for he stopped every movement in an instant of intent listening. He got up and turned about. Joy and excitement once more brought that flash of a miracle and for a fleeting second old Alexis Dahlberg was young Alexis Dahlberg again. Thus do the old partake of the happiness and even of the very youth of those who are dear to them.

It was much as it had always been when Chris came up the valley from the Anderson farm. He would sit down by the hearth exchanging with Grandfather the news of all things which each one had seen and done since last they met. In his own place and under his own roof, Chris never had any want of words. They came now in a plunging torrent.

"Begin at the beginning," Grandfather was obliged

to tell him half a dozen times. "Do you think my slow wits can follow you while you leap from Goose Wing River to St. Louis in a breath? And what is this Lone Tree Crossing you keep talking of? You have not even told me yet, what is a crossing of any kind."

Before twilight fell, however, he interrupted the tale to lead Chris outside to the brow of the hill where once had stood the great walnut tree. There in its place was set a little green sapling, small but lusty, growing with vigorous energy.

"In a hundred years it may perhaps have to be cut again," observed Grandfather reflectively, "but that is no long time. Can you look afar over these mountains and rivers and say that it is any great matter, the mere passing of a hundred years over the head of my little nut tree?"

They sat on the doorstone while night descended softly upon them. Talk ceased for a little and Chris, in silence, watched the dusk walk all abroad through the forest. Whatever had been accomplished by that long journey, great things or small, this was what brought him the greatest happiness, to feel that he was at home again after long wayfaring, to see the darkness come down all about him and to know that it covered only safe, well-beloved and familiar things.

THE END